Little Plum

Rumer Godden was one of the UK's most distinguished authors. She wrote many well-known and much-loved books for both adults and children, including *The Dolls' House*, *The Story of Holly & Ivy* and *The Diddakoi*, which won the Whitbread Children's Book Award in 1972.

She was awarded the OBE in 1993 and died in 1998, aged ninety.

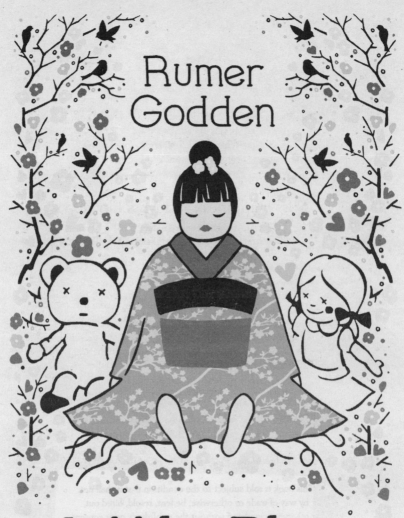

Rumer Godden

Little Plum

Illustrated by Sarah Gibb

MACMILLAN CHILDREN'S BOOKS

First published 1963 by Macmillan London Limited

This edition published 2015 by Macmillan Children's Books
an imprint of Pan Macmillan
20 New Wharf Road, London N1 9RR
Associated companies throughout the world
www.panmacmillan.com

ISBN 978-1-4472-9276-0

Printed and bound by CPI Group (UK) Ltd, Croydon CR0 4YY

Contents

Chapter 1

Once upon a time there were two little Japanese dolls whose names were Miss Happiness and Miss Flower. They belonged to a girl called Nona Fell and they were her dearest possessions. Long ago – 'Nearly a year ago,' said Nona – when she had first come from India to live in Topmeadow with her cousins, the dolls had arrived too in a Christmas parcel from Great-Aunt Lucy Dickinson. No one

knew anything about them but their names, which were written on a piece of paper in Great-Aunt Lucy Dickinson's spidery handwriting, but the two foreign little dolls had looked as forlorn, cold and homesick as Nona herself. In settling them in she had somehow settled herself.

Miss Happiness and Miss Flower were only five inches high; they were made of white plaster, their bodies of rag but, as Nona said, they were people. Even Nona's cousin Tom admitted that. Their eyes were slits of black glass, they had delicate plaster noses and red painted mouths. Their hair was real, black and straight, cut in a fringe. Miss Flower was a little taller and thinner, Miss Happiness's cheeks were fatter and her red mouth was painted in a smile. Both of them wore kimonos and had a sash high under their arms, folded over into a heavy pad at the back. On their feet were painted sandals. When this story begins they had not met Little Plum. In any case her story begins with the children – Nona and her cousins, Anne, Tom and Belinda – their surname was Fell too – it begins with the children and the House Next Door.

Nona and Belinda's bedroom windows looked straight into the House Next Door. The children always called it that because it had no name, besides it was so very much next door that its windows and the Fells' had only a few yards between them. That was the Fells' fault, as Father said. Two years ago they had to build on to their house. 'When we bought it,' said Father – long, long ago when Anne was a baby – 'we didn't know we were going to have all of you!' A playroom had been built and over it two bedrooms for Nona and Belinda to have as their own, and it was this that brought the two houses so close. There was a hedge between them, though it was not very high, and there was, of course, the ilex tree. It was the only ilex in the road and the Fells were proud of it – a great old tree that was almost evergreen because the old leaves only dropped when the next ones were ready to take their place in August. It grew between the back corner of the Fells' house and the House Next Door. Its trunk was in the Fells' garden but its roots and its branches had spread; indeed, some of these almost tapped the next-door upstairs windows. 'But it belongs to us,' said Belinda jealously. Father had wanted to lop its branches, or even to cut it down, but Mother would not let him. 'It's beautiful,' she said, 'and it does give both houses a little privacy.'

Mother and Father did not really like the House Next Door being so close, but Belinda and Nona liked to look into the rooms over the way. 'But I wish there was somebody in them,' said Belinda.

It had been empty for a long, long time and the windows had slowly become so dirty that the children could not see past them, while the roses that grew up the wall had twined right over them. 'It's getting derelict,' said Mother. Derelict means shabby, forgotten, falling to bits, and it was sad that the House Next Door must become that. 'Why doesn't somebody buy it?' asked Belinda.

'I expect the price is too high,' said Father.

'And I expect it would take a lot of money,' said Mother, 'to keep up a house like that.'

It was true that the Fells' house and garden would have fitted into half of the gracious white house that had a garden in front with a lawn and flower-beds and a gravel drive round them, and a big garden behind.

'There are eighteen windows just in its front – I counted,' said Belinda. 'And in our house live Mother and Father, Anne, Tom, Nona and me – six people,' which was not counting Mrs Bodger who came to clean every day, while in the House Next Door lived no one at all.

'Poor house, becoming derelict,' said Nona.

Nona was nine years old, a dark, thin child. Belinda was eight, a rough, tough little girl with curly fair hair. Anne was fifteen, Tom twelve. Anne, Tom and Belinda had lived in Topmeadow all their lives. It was the suburb of a country market

town, not far from London, and it was pretty, with wide streets, houses with gardens, old cottages. It still had its village High Street and its great park, as English villages have, though the park belonged to the town now. The children thought it the best place in the world to live in and it seemed a waste that the House Next Door should be empty.

Then one September morning Belinda was late. That was not uncommon; she by no means always got up when she was told, and this morning, leaving out washing, not doing up her zip, or tying her shoe laces, she had just pulled her jersey over her head and was giving a hasty brush to her hair when she stopped, the brush still in her hand; a lorry had drawn up at the gate of the House Next Door and men in overalls with ladders, planks and buckets were getting out. Belinda watched while the men came up the path and one of them took a key out of his pocket and opened the front door. Then she saw another thing. A second man had planted a notice board by the hedge. Belinda read it and then, with the brush still in her hand, she tumbled down the stairs and burst into the dining room.

'Guess what?' she shouted. 'The House Next Door is sold.'

Mother, Anne, Tom, Nona all looked up at her

but Father only turned over a page of his newspaper, and said, 'Didn't I tell you? It was sold a month ago.'

'Father!' said Belinda, and they all bombarded him with questions.

'What's their name?'

'Who are they?'

'When are they coming?'

'Where do they come from?'

And Belinda beseeched, 'Have they any children? Have they?'

Father read a little more, ate another piece of toast, drank a little coffee, while Belinda danced in her chair with impatience. When at last he did speak, all he said was: 'I suggest, Belinda, you do up your zip.'

Belinda did up her zip.

'And your shoe laces.'

Belinda tied her laces.

'And go upstairs and finish brushing your hair. Yes, and you might wash your face,' Father called up after her. 'I can see you had cocoa last night for supper.'

When Belinda came down, neat and tidy, Father had turned another page. She had to wait, but at last he said, 'I believe their name is Jones.'

'That's a good ordinary name,' said Mother.

'Ah, but they are not ordinary Joneses, they are Tiffany Joneses.'

A double-barrelled name, but it sounded most impressive; in fact, she could hardly say it. 'Stiffany Jones,' she said the first time.

'Tiffany Jones,' Nona corrected her, and then said thoughtfully, 'It makes Fell seem very plain.'

'He has mines in the Far East; firms in Burma and Japan,' said Father.

'It sounds rich,' said Nona.

'They must be rich,' said Belinda, 'to pay the high price.'

'We don't think about whether people are rich or not,' said Mother, which was not entirely true. Nona and Belinda were to think about it a great deal in the weeks to come, but now there was something else in which they were far more interested.

'Have they any children?' Belinda asked again.

Chapter 2

The House Next Door was made new. 'And how new!' said Belinda. All that autumn other boards appeared: Mason and Perry Ltd, Builders; Goss and Gomm, Central Heating; Palmer Green Ltd, Electrical Engineers. Men swarmed in and over the house from the garden to the roof, and the whole road was filled with the sound of knocking and hammering. A concrete mixer turned. Rubble and old wood, pulled-out fireplaces, pipes, cooking stove and cisterns were dumped on the lawn. Lorries came and went; the gas people arrived and a telephone van; and the pavement was taken up. Soon the ilex was covered with dust, and more dust with smells and noise came over the hedge into the Fells' house. Mother said it was almost unbearable, but Belinda loved it. She and Nona watched all day, every day, and every day they had something new to report.

'It gets intresinger and intresinger,' said Belinda.

A fireplace with a white mantel went in; 'Marble,' Nona told Belinda. The floors were sanded with a machine that made the worst noise and dust of all. Then they were repolished. Doors and windows, skirting and banisters were painted white. 'The House Next Door has two staircases,' said Belinda. She went in and out and had made friends with the workmen, but Nona was too shy; she only watched.

Then other new boards appeared: Martin Moresby, Decorators, and Hall, Jones and Hall, Perfect Landscape Gardeners. Belinda was not allowed in any more; pale satined wallpapers went up, new carpets were laid in every room and on the stairs.

'Must have cost a fortune,' said Belinda.

'Not a *fortune*,' Anne corrected her, but Belinda nodded her head.

'I heard the men say so.' Belinda might not be able to go in but she could still look and listen. 'Saucers and pitchers', Father called Belinda's eyes and ears.

The landscape gardeners tidied the garden, pruned, cleared and weeded; made new paved walks where the old brick paths had been and dug new flower-beds. The lawns were dug up too, smoothed and turfed and rolled, their edges trimmed. The roses round the windows were cut back, and the flower-beds were filled with new plants bearing labels with strange sounding names: 'Cystisus albus?' asked Belinda; 'Viburnum sterile?' Nona wrote them down and took them to her friend, old Mr Twilfit who kept the bookshop.

Nona was often in and out of the bookshop, and sometimes she took Miss Happiness and Miss Flower to visit Mr Twilfit. 'You see, he helped to establish them,' she said. He had lent her books on Japan so that she could learn to play with them properly, he had helped design the dolls' house, 'and

12

he has given me all sorts of things,' said Nona.

He was a surprising friend of Nona, who was a timid child. 'She was brought up in India away from people, and that made her shy,' Belinda often explained. Most children were afraid of Mr Twilfit; he had a bad temper, a habit of roaring in his deep voice and his eyebrows looked ferocious; 'grey caterpillars', Belinda called them. Even she was quiet when she went with Nona to the bookshop, quiet and very respectful; 'Mr Twilfit must be very wise, with all those books,' she said.

'Silly, he doesn't read them,' said Tom. 'He sells them.'

'He reads a lot of them,' said Nona, 'and Belinda's right. He is wise; the wisest man I know.' When there was anything Nona wanted to know she always went and asked Mr Twilfit.

'Cystisus albus?' he said now. 'That's a pearly white broom. Viburnum sterile? That's a snowball tree.'

'Why couldn't they say so?' asked Belinda.

Even the garage was made new, big enough

for three cars, and given doors that opened by themselves if you pressed a button, which seemed magical to Belinda; the garage had a new glass roof too, over its courtyard.

'That's for the chauffeur to wash the cars under when it rains,' said Tom.

'Will they have a chauffeur?' asked Belinda, impressed.

'Sure to; and I expect he will live in the flat over the garage. It's being made new too,' said Tom.

The Tiffany Joneses, it seemed, left nothing to chance. Burglar alarms were fitted to all the doors and the downstairs windows.

'Well, they probably have valuable things,' said Anne. Then the fire escapes with curly iron steps were built each side of the house; the one on the Fells' side was close beside the ilex tree, almost touched by its branches.

'I hope they won't ask us to lop it,' said Anne.

'They will probably like the way it screens their garden from us,' said Mother.

At last, just at Christmas time, the House Next

Door was ready, spick and span, in fact so spick and span it made one catch one's breath.

'Just imagine if you left finger marks on that white paint,' said Anne.

'If you brought in a bit of mud on those floors,' said Tom, while Mother said she would hardly dare to cook in the white tiled, blue and white kitchen. The garden too was uncomfortably tidy.

'Suppose a ball went into one of those shrubs,' said Tom.

'If you fell off your scooter into one of the beds,' said Belinda, 'or rode your bicycle on the paths and went on to the new grass.'

'You couldn't ride your bicycle in that garden,' said Nona, 'or scooter.'

'I don't think there *can* be any children,' said Belinda, but when two days after Christmas the furniture arrived, Belinda and Nona saw what was unmistakably children's furniture – and what beautiful furniture it was. There was a pale blue bed with poles, like a four-poster, with a pale blue dressing table, chest of drawers and chairs to match. There was furniture too, for a sitting room: a school desk, a blackboard, small armchairs, bookcases and, delivered in a special van, a miniature white piano. There were toys: a big dolls' house, dolls' beds, a doll's perambulator almost as large as a real one, a cooking stove, a pale blue bicycle, and all of them were obviously for a girl.

Tom groaned. 'We have enough girls already.'

'I think,' said Belinda, 'there must be four or five, there are so many toys.'

'But there's only one bed,' said Nona.

To their great excitement, all these were carried into the two rooms that were opposite Nona and Belinda's bedrooms.

'That's where the girl is going to sleep and play,' said Belinda. 'What fun! We shall be able to watch her and wave to her.'

'If she will wave to us,' said Nona, but such a doubt never entered Belinda's head.

Not long after the furniture, a lady and gentleman arrived.

'In . . . is it a Rolls-Royce?' whispered Belinda.

'A Phantom Silver Cloud II,' said Tom, 'and brand new.'

It was grey and black with dark grey leather. A gentleman was driving with a lady beside him, and a chauffeur in a grey uniform was sitting behind.

The big car stopped at the gate: the chauffeur sprang out to open the door, but the gentleman was already out and, 'Is that the father?' whispered Belinda. 'He doesn't look like a father.'

He was certainly not like any of the fathers she had ever seen: he was young, tall, thin, pale and far more . . . 'elegant,' said Nona. She and Belinda, little girls as they were, could see he was beautifully dressed. 'I never thought of a man's clothes being beautiful before,' said Nona afterwards. 'His trousers had edges,' whispered Belinda. She meant their creases were sharply pressed. His shirt seemed to be cream coloured silk, his shoes shone, his dark overcoat looked warm and rich, and Nona thought with a pang of her uncle's raincoat, his office suit, his old tweed coat and flannels. Mr Tiffany Jones was wearing what Belinda called a city hat, from seeing men who wore them catching the morning train to London. 'It's a bowler hat,' said Nona.

The lady looked older than he; tall too, but large, in a large fur coat, high-heeled fur boots and a red velvet hat. Her face was red too, 'red and white,' said Belinda.

'Hush! That's rouge and powder,' said Nona.

'Does she think it looks nice?' asked Belinda.

The lady had a string of pearls, and a diamond watch over her glove. Belinda and Nona saw it sparkle as she lifted her hand and, 'I can smell her from here,' said Belinda.

After the Rolls-Royce came another, smaller car and in it were two women who wore white overalls under their coats; it was driven by a man who soon afterward appeared in a striped jacket. 'A butler,' said Nona, but Mother said he was more likely to be a house-man. The children could see them through the windows, hurrying about, moving furniture, carrying things, while the lady stood in the middle of each room in turn, ordering everyone about.

The gentleman stayed out in the garden, walking about the lawn, looking at the flower-beds as if he did not like them very much. Every now and again he read one of the labels, and seemed as surprised as Nona and Belinda had been at their names.

He heard Belinda's loud voice and looked up, saw them behind the hedge and smiled. Even to the children it seemed a sad and absent-minded smile and, I wonder what's the matter with him, thought Nona.

The front door opened. 'Harold! Harold!' the lady called in an imperious voice that was louder even than Belinda's. 'Harold! You might come and help.'

'My dear Agnes, I thought I should only be in the way.'

'It's your house!' said the lady.

'Then isn't it hers? Isn't she Mrs Tiffany Jones?' asked Belinda.

It seemed that she was not. The new cook had made friends with Mrs Bodger and soon the Fells knew all about the Tiffany Joneses. 'With Mrs Bodger and Belinda, who could help it?' as Father said. The real Mrs Tiffany Jones, it seemed, was in hospital because two years ago she had caught polio.

'Polio . . . that's the illness when you can't move, isn't it?' asked Belinda. She tried to imagine what that would be like. 'It would be terrible,' said Belinda, awed.

'Polio often does paralyse,' said Mother. 'How very, very sad.'

'She got it in London,' Belinda reported, 'and Miss Tiffany Jones had to come and look after the house there, and look after the girl.' Mrs Bodger had said there was one little girl. 'Look after her,' said Belinda, 'because Mr often goes travelling, but

now Mrs Tiffany Jones had been sent to . . . to . . .'
Belinda could not remember the name and said, 'to
a famous hospital there.'

'Of course, Stoke Mandeville,' said Mother,
which was not far from Topmeadow. 'That's where
they teach people to move again; walk and swim
and use wheelchairs. Perhaps it means she is getting
better.'

'He bought the House Next Door just to be
near her – this great big house,' said Belinda. 'Miss
Tiffany Jones has come here too, and will look after
it. She's his sister, his much older sister. She used to
look after him when he was a little boy. That's why
he can't say "boo!" to her.'

'Belinda, you are not to repeat gossip,' said
Mother.

'It isn't gossip. He can't,' said Belinda. 'Their cook
told Mrs Bodger.'

'Then Miss Tiffany Jones is the little girl's aunt,'
said Nona. 'I don't think I would like her for my
aunt.'

'She's a proper old cat,' said Belinda.

'*Belinda!*' Mother was horrified.

'But she is, Cook told Mrs Bodger so.'

The cook's name was Mrs Mount; the other maid was Eileen. The house-man was called Selwyn, 'and you don't call him Mister,' said Belinda. The chauffeur was Benson; 'you don't call him Mister, either.' They were all complete except for the little girl.

Then, on a bitter January day, the Rolls drew up at the next-door gate and out got a girl and a woman. Belinda and Nona, who were just coming back from the shops, clutched one another.

The girl walking up the path looked about the same age as Nona. She was wearing a green velvet coat and hat, white boots, fur-topped, and white fur tippet, white gloves and a white shawl wound round her neck and over her mouth. 'As well as the tippet!' said Belinda.

The girl was as pale as Mr Tiffany Jones, and down her back hung a long fall of fair hair. It gave her the look of being drowned, thought Nona.

She and Belinda looked to where the woman was taking a rug and parcels from the chauffeur. She was a big solid-looking woman with a big face and iron-grey hair, and she was dressed in an iron-grey coat and hat. 'She looks iron all over,' said Nona.

'Is she the nurse?' asked Belinda in a whisper. 'That girl's too old to have a nurse. That must be a governess.'

'She doesn't look like a governess,' said Nona uncertainly. 'Perhaps she's a kind of maid.'

Miss Tiffany Jones had come out on the steps to meet them. 'Come in! Come in! Come along in!' she called in her imperious voice. 'Hurry up, Matson,' she called to the woman. As with Selwyn and Benson, Miss Tiffany Jones did not say Mrs or Miss. It seemed rude to Belinda to call people by their surnames, but 'Come along, Matson. Hurry up out of the cold,' called Miss Tiffany Jones.

'They are coming as fast as they can,' murmured

Belinda. She and Nona had gone into their own garden and were looking through the hedge.

Selwyn came out to carry the suitcases. 'Welcome home, Miss Gem,' he said respectfully as if he were talking to a grown-up.

'Jem; that's a boy's name,' said Belinda.

'Not J-E-M, silly; G-E-M,' said Tom, who had come up behind them.

'Never heard of it,' said Belinda, as if she had heard of everything.

'It certainly goes well with Tiffany,' said Mr Twilfit when he heard it. Nona and Belinda had gone down to the bookshop to tell him that Gem had arrived. Tiffany's, he explained to them, was a famous jeweller's and goldsmith's in New York. 'Does it belong to Gem's father?' asked Belinda, her eyes round.

'Hardly probable,' said Mr Twilfit; 'might be some connection, though.'

'I think "Gem" is a pretty name,' said Nona.

'Gem Tiffany Jones. It's the richest name I ever heard.'

*

'Belinda,' said Mother a day or two later. 'Belinda, you are not to go next door.'

'Oh Mother, why not? Mr Tiffany Jones smiles at us.'

'I know,' said Mother, 'But Miss Tiffany Jones doesn't.'

Mother had spoken to Miss Tiffany Jones when she met her in the road. 'I hope you are going to like living in Topmeadow.'

'After London?' Miss Tiffany Jones gave a queer little laugh that did not sound amused. 'Like living in a *suburb*, and not even a London suburb?'

'But Topmeadow's a lovely place,' said Belinda.

Miss Tiffany Jones did not speak to Mother again, nor nod to any of them or smile, and, 'You are not to go next door,' said Mother to Belinda.

'Which means not hanging round the gate,' said Anne, and Belinda blushed.

'I want to make friends,' said Belinda.

Belinda was friends with everyone: with the shop people, the postman, the laundryman, the Vicar;

with Sir William Mortimer who was Topmeadow's Member of Parliament and with the old chestnut seller who had his stand in winter at the corner of the road.

Nona had only three friends, and she had made them through Miss Happiness and Miss Flower. Nona was friends with Melly, the girl she sat next to at school, Miss Lane who taught there, and Mr Twilfit.

These were Nona's friends, but to Belinda everyone was a friend, and it was an astonishing idea to her for the Fells not to make friends at once with the Tiffany Joneses, but Mother was quite firm.

'You are not to go next door, Belinda.'

'What? Never?' asked Belinda.

'Not unless you are asked,' said Mother.

'But suppose they never ask me?'

'Then you can never go,' said Tom.

Chapter 3

The weather grew colder and colder, until one day snow began to fall. It fell all the morning and by the afternoon the road, the roofs and gardens, the whole of Topmeadow, was white with snow. Then the sky cleared, the sun came out, the frost sparkled and Nona brought Miss Happiness and Miss Flower out to see the snowy world. The dolls wore warm coats over their kimonos, coats wadded and quilted with cotton wool. Over their painted sandals they had warm white socks and Tom had made them tiny clogs, cut

from a cork and tied on with cords of embroidery cotton. Their heads were protected by round flat hats tied under their chins. Nona brought them down as far as the low wall that bounded the Fells' garden from the road; she made them walk up and down along the wall; their feet left footprints in the snow, smaller than a bird's.

Belinda came to look. 'What are you doing, Nona?'

'Miss Happiness and Miss Flower have come out to admire the snow.'

'Is that what they do in Japan?'

'My book says so.'

'You might have told me,' said Belinda. 'I would have brought Little Peach.'

Little Peach was a Japanese boy baby doll, no bigger than my thumb. He had come to Belinda in a peach as Peach Boy in the Japanese fairy tale had come (the fairy tale of Little Peach or Peach Boy can be found in every Japanese fairy-story book). Now Belinda ran up to her bedroom and fetched him. Little Peach's hair was cut round, his legs were

curved like a baby's and he had
no clothes; Belinda had lost
his coat and trousers
and had not had
time to make
him any more –
Belinda never had
enough time – but
she had wrapped
him in a handkerchief. Now, 'You keep him,' she
said to Nona.

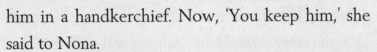

Nona was used to keeping Little Peach – Belinda
always had so many other things to do – and now
Nona tied him on Miss Flower's back in the way
that Japanese girls often carry their baby brothers.
She had just begun to make them walk up and down
the wall again, when the next door gate opened and
out came Mr Tiffany Jones. He stopped when he
saw them, then came closer, bending his height
down to look. 'How very pretty,' said Mr Tiffany
Jones, gazing down at Miss Happiness, Miss Flower
and Little Peach. 'May I touch?' And when Nona

shyly nodded, he picked up Miss Happiness.

'Why, you have made them tanzen – proper Japanese coats – and tabi,' he said, touching the socks. Tabi means 'footbag' in Japanese and tabi are like bags with one toe for the big toe. Nona, of course, had not been able to separate the dolls' toes but their warm white socks did look like tiny bags.

'Lucky little dolls, they are beautifully warm,' said Mr Tiffany Jones, gently putting Miss Happiness down. 'What are they called?'

Nona told him their names and, 'They have come out to admire the snow,' Belinda explained. 'Japanese people do.'

'So they do,' said Mr Tiffany Jones. 'And I believe they make up poems about it – or say one,' and, standing in the road in all his elegance, Mr Tiffany Jones recited:

'All heaven and earth
is flowered white,
hidden in snow,
unceasing snow.'

'Why, that's a haiku!' cried Nona, delighted. A haiku is one of the smallest Japanese poems, only seventeen syllables long, just right for dolls, and if Miss Happiness's and Miss Flower's little plaster faces could have smiled, they would have given the honourable gentleman a smile and they would have bowed to him – Japanese people bow a great deal, and they speak of people as 'honourable'.

'How do *you* know about Japanese things?' said Belinda to Mr Tiffany Jones. 'Nona knows, and Mr Twilfit, but how do you?'

'Well, I go to Japan sometimes,' said Mr Tiffany Jones. 'As a matter of fact, I'm going there tomorrow for three or four days.'

'Did he say three or four days?' asked Belinda, when he had gone on down the road. 'But . . . Japan's on the other side of the world.'

'Nowadays people fly all over the world very quickly,' Nona told her, and Father said that too. Mr Tiffany Jones, Father said, was an important person in business. 'He might very well fly to Japan for just one meeting,' said Father.

Before Mr Tiffany Jones had walked away, he had bent down and picked Miss Flower up to look at her. 'Charming,' he said, touching Miss Flower's red hat with a gentle finger, and, 'I wish my little girl could play like this,' he said, and he had not sounded important, only wistful.

'You know,' said Mother a few days afterwards, 'I am beginning to feel sorry for that little girl.'

'What little girl?' Nona and Belinda did not quite follow Mother. 'What little girl?'

'Gem; I'm sorry for her.'

'*Sorry!* For *Gem?*'

'Yes,' said Mother.

'But . . . she has *everything*,' said Nona.

'*Look* at the things she has,' said Belinda.

One thing that particularly filled Belinda with envy was Gem's pony. Almost every day the riding master from the stables near the Park would ride up to the House Next Door, and beside his horse trotted a white pony, glossy white, with a long white mane and tail, the daintiest pony imaginable. 'Half Arab, he told me so,' said Belinda.

The pony had a new saddle and bridle with a scarlet headband, a white sheepskin under the saddle; 'And he's Gem's *own*. They just keep him at the stables. If I had a pony like that,' said Belinda, 'I would be happy forever.'

'Would you, I wonder,' said Mother, 'if you had to be Gem?'

When Nona and Belinda came to think of it, Gem did lead a queer restricted life. Belinda tried to imagine what it would be like not to be free to run in and out of the house and garden. Gem was older than Belinda, but she was not even allowed to run as far as the pillar-box at the corner to post a letter; Selwyn posted the letters. She never went on errands to the shops as Belinda loved to go. 'They give me sweets and apples,' said Belinda, and Mr Hancock, the fishmonger, sometimes let her ring up the cash register for him. Gem never went to the Park to meet other children for games – she walked there beside Matson – and Mr Tiffany Jones was right, she never seemed to play. 'Why doesn't she play?' asked Belinda. 'He said he wished she could. Why doesn't she?'

Nona did not know but, 'Perhaps she needs a Japanese doll,' said Miss Happiness and Miss Flower. They could talk to one another but, of course, nobody else could hear.

The children had discovered that Matson was Gem's especial maid. 'A maid for what?' asked Belinda.

'To keep her rooms tidy,' suggested Anne.

'Doesn't she have to tidy them herself?'

That made Belinda envious.

'And to look after her clothes,' said Anne.

'Does she have so many clothes?'

That was another thing: Gem never seemed to wear the comfortable, ordinary clothes Nona and Belinda wore – jeans, or shorts and jerseys, an anorak with a hood, a kilted skirt, hair tied up in a ponytail. 'She's always dressed up,' said Belinda; dressed in elaborate dresses with ruffled petticoats, in coats with white collars or trimmed with fur, in tailored suits. For riding, Gem wore jodhpurs, a white silk shirt, yellow waistcoat, smart tweed jacket, velvet cap and dear little jodhpur boots.

She had fur-trimmed boots and hats, spotless white gloves, and she had a real fur coat, 'like a lady's, only little,' reported Belinda.

More and more Gem seemed like a girl in a book, 'and not a very truthful book,' said Nona, because nowadays not even princes and princesses were treated like this. 'Princesses have to be friendly and smile and wave,' said Belinda. Gem never smiled or waved; like her aunt, she did not seem to want to know the Fells. They never saw her stand at her windows and watch Nona's and Belinda's or peer through the hedge as they did. If she met them on the road she looked the other way. Of course, she may not have been free to wave or smile; everywhere she went Matson followed her, 'like a policeman,' said Belinda. 'Only, policemen are nice,' said Nona. Soon Nona and Belinda found themselves saying, 'Poor Gem.' How odd it was that Gem should be poor when she was so very rich.

Mr Tiffany Jones came back from Japan and, 'Did he bring the little Miss a Japanese doll?' Miss Happiness and Miss Flower asked anxiously. No, it seemed he had only brought Gem a Japanese lantern. It was a beautiful lantern, big, of misty white paper with a black band top and bottom; when it was lit it glowed

yellow. Nona, Belinda and the dolls could see it hanging up in Gem's sitting-room window; it looked most poetical – but Miss Happiness and Miss Flower were curiously disappointed.

Belinda's best present at Christmas had been a pair of roller skates. Up till then she had used Tom's old ones, dreadful ones that had the old kind of steel wheels, 'horribly noisy,' said Anne, and were rigid, without ball bearings, the grips worn out. They were always coming off and bringing Belinda down. The new ones were beautiful, with leather heel grips, ball bearings and hard rubber rollers; they were swift, almost noiseless, and on them Belinda felt she flew. 'But if they are fast, they can be dangerous,' Mother told her. 'You can go as fast as you like in the Park or round the tennis court, but you are not to go fast on the road.' She let the children skate on the pavement of their own road because it was quiet, but they were not allowed to go up to the shops at its end; Mother did not know that they often skated round the corner into the next road that led to the Park. 'You may skate slowly, on our pavement, but if you go fast, I shall have to stop it,' said Mother.

On those new skates, Belinda could not help going fast – at least, she could not resist it. Besides, she and Tom had a secret game: they raced on opposite pavements, each side of the road. Tom gave Belinda a start and they skated to the far end, away from the shops, and back again to the house. Tom had to turn round a pillar-box at the corner of his pavement, Belinda round a lamppost. They both went furiously fast. 'But only when we see the road is empty,' said Tom. 'Or almost empty,' said Belinda, who was not as careful as Tom. 'One or two people don't matter.'

Sometimes they did matter. Once one of the people was Miss Tiffany Jones. Belinda had not realized who she was, and shot past her, making Miss Tiffany Jones almost jump out of her skin. 'Child! You must not skate like that, on a public road,' she cried. Belinda, dragging her skate sideways, had managed to stop.

'How dare you!' scolded Miss Tiffany Jones. 'I don't know where you come from – ' she seemed curiously blind to the Fells next door – 'but if I see you again, I shall tell the police. Why! You might give someone a heart attack!'

Scarlet in the face, her head sheepishly down, Belinda skated slowly away and stole in at her own gate, and for two whole days she did not skate on the road at all. She even carried her skates to the Park, but Belinda was not very old, and when you are young, you forget. Besides, by far the most exciting place for skating was the road. On the third day she was back again, but she kept a wary eye out for Miss Tiffany Jones.

'There's ice on the roads,' said Father next morning at breakfast. 'Be careful how you walk.'

'And how you skate,' said Mother. 'Better keep off the road, Belinda. If you get a patch of ice, you might skid and not be able to stop.'

'I can always stop,' said Belinda, 'and if I can't, it's more fun.'

'Not fun for other people,' said Anne.

'Oh, I can always dodge them,' said Belinda airily.

It was wonderful skating that day. Tom and Belinda stayed in the Park all the morning; it was almost lunchtime when they came back, and the pavements were empty. They were on the road leading to their own, and 'Let's race home,' said Belinda.

'What about the corner?' asked Tom. The corner to their own road was sharp.

'Oh, there won't be anybody there,' said Belinda. 'We can swing round the lamppost.'

'All right. Give you forty yards to start,' said Tom,

and when they were stationed, 'Ready! Steady! GO!' called Tom.

Belinda's skates were so good and she was skating so well, that she was able to keep well ahead of Tom. She could hear him, though, coming behind her and, 'I'm going to get there first,' she said through her teeth. The air was so cold and she was going so fast that her cheeks stung and her eyes were watering, but – faster – faster – faster – thought Belinda.

She reached the corner, swung round the lamppost to turn, but did not really look as she gathered speed again; nor did she listen or she would have heard Tom grind to a halt and shout, 'Look out! Belinda, look out!'

Then suddenly in front of her she saw the Tiffany Joneses, Mr, Miss and Gem, their backs towards her, walking towards their front gate. They were strung so much across the pavement, that there was no room for Belinda to pass. She tried to brake, but she was going too fast; she tried to steer towards the wall, and met exactly what Mother had warned her about, a patch of ice. The skates flew sideways, she spun round twice and, pell-mell, crash, went into the back of Gem and sent her flying. Worse than that, skidding after her, Belinda lost her own balance, veered backwards and forwards, clutching Gem; the skates flew up, one roller catching Mr Tiffany Jones on the shin where he had whipped round to look. Then Belinda fell flat on her back on the ice, bringing Gem down on top of her.

What a to-do there was! Mr Tiffany Jones was hopping on one leg, swearing with pain; his black striped trousers had a great rip. Miss Tiffany Jones was half crying with shock and scolding in her high, loud voice. Tom, who had rushed up, was picking up Gem as well as he could with his skates on, trying to clean her coat from mud and ice, while he told Belinda under his breath what he thought of her. Gem's white fur hat was lying in the road, her muff was dangling on one string, the gold-green hair was draggled with ice and mud, and she was silent and white. 'She might have said something,' said Belinda afterwards. 'Well, you knocked the breath out of her,' said Tom.

He left Gem to Miss Tiffany Jones and dragged Belinda to her feet. Belinda was too ashamed and shocked to say a word then, but Tom apologized, though Miss Tiffany Jones hardly paused long enough to hear him. 'A perfect little hooligan,' she was saying. 'I told her only the other day not to skate like this; she must be severely punished,' she told Tom.

'It was partly my fault,' said Tom. 'I let her race.'

'Then you should be thoroughly ashamed of yourself.'

'Oh come, Agnes! It was an accident,' said Mr Tiffany Jones, who was beginning to recover, 'and Gem isn't hurt.'

42

'Accident! Not hurt! The child looks stunned and sick.' Then Miss Tiffany Jones turned again on Belinda. 'Using the streets as a skating rink! You are a public danger. I would telephone your mother, but as she lets you play in the streets, I doubt it would do much good.'

She swept Gem in at the gate; Mr Tiffany Jones said, 'She will calm down by and by,' and smiled and followed her. Tom took Belinda home. He was given a good talking to and both their skates were confiscated for a week.

Mother wrote a note of apology to Miss Tiffany Jones and made Belinda, who could not bear writing letters, write one to Gem. This was a real punishment for Belinda, and even when she had written it three times there were still blots. 'I bet Gem writes *beautifully*,' she said, but that they could not know, because Gem did not answer; nor did Miss Tiffany Jones.

'That's not very gracious of them,' said Father.

Mr Tiffany Jones still lifted his hat when he met Mother in the street – 'And he lifts it to me,' said

Anne – he still smiled with his wistful smile, and said, 'Hullo Tornado,' in a most friendly way when he met Belinda, but Miss Tiffany Jones swept by with her head in the air. As for Gem, she walked straight past. 'She thinks I did it on purpose,' said Belinda resentfully.

'I'm sure she doesn't,' said Mother.

'Then she might at least smile,' said Belinda. 'Anyone can smile.'

'Do you smile at her?' asked Mother.

'Certainly not,' said Belinda. 'But why are the Tiffany Joneses like this? Why?' she asked Mother.

'Different people have different ideas,' said Mother, 'and bring their children up differently.'

'Not as differently as this,' said Belinda.

'Remember Topmeadow is a new place for them,' said Nona. 'Remember how silly I was when I first came.'

'You were miserable,' said Belinda, 'but you weren't stuck up.' Then a thought struck her. The holidays were almost over. 'Soon it will be time for school,' said Belinda. 'Gem will have to go to school. *That* will unstick her.'

But when term time came Gem did not go to school.

Instead, a number of new people came to the House Next Door. A lady came every day from half past nine until one; she was a proper governess and her name, the children discovered, was Miss Berryman. The Mademoiselle from their own school came twice a week to teach Gem French privately. 'But she knows French already,' said Belinda. 'She can talk it.' This was a mystery to Belinda, who was still struggling with 'avoir' and 'être'. A gentleman came on three afternoons at half past four to teach Gem the piano. 'And she has to practise a whole hour every day,' said Belinda. They could hear her on the little white piano and, 'She's very good,' said Anne, 'better than I am and I'm twice her age.' Gem learned elocution and had private dancing lessons, 'ballet, twice a week,' said Nona, longingly.

There seemed a great many lessons for one small girl. 'Chivvied from morning to night – that's what she is,' Belinda reported in the words of Mrs Bodger.

'Nothing but putting clothes on and taking them off, and practising and lessons, lessons, lessons.'

Mother was disturbed by this. 'Every child should have some private time,' she said, 'time of her own and time for play.' Perhaps Mr Tiffany Jones felt this too. When Mother took Belinda to buy a new satchel – Belinda's first grown-up satchel; before she had only had an old one of Anne's – and they met Mr and Miss Tiffany Jones, 'Getting ready for school?' he asked pleasantly.

'School has started,' said Belinda, who was amazed that anyone living in Topmeadow should not know that.

'I didn't know,' said Mr Tiffany Jones as if he had guessed what Belinda was thinking. 'You see,' he said, 'Gem doesn't go to school.'

'Not at Topmeadow,'Miss Tiffany Jones broke in. 'Gem is a very gifted child,' she said; 'she couldn't go to an *ordinary* school. Come, Harold,' and she put her hand on Mr Tiffany Jones's arm and marched him away.

Nona had made Miss Happiness and Miss Flower

go to school too. 'A school by themselves', and she said, 'I wish they knew another Japanese child.' She had made tiny writing books for the dolls, bound in the Japanese way, pleated into pages that can be opened out into one long scroll; you begin on the last page and work back to the first. Japanese characters are written with a brush and not a pen; Nona made the smallest possible brushes from a splinter of a match and a piece of feather, and copied some Japanese characters on to a dolls'-house blackboard for the dolls to copy and write. Japanese is such a different language that in Japan children spend all their time learning to read and write, but she made each of the dolls learn a haiku too. 'One day you shall say them to honourable Mr Tiffany Jones,' she told them, and the dolls felt pleased. Miss Happiness's haiku was:

'You stupid scarecrow!
Under your very
stick feet
Birds are stealing beans.'

While Miss Flower's was this:

> 'Gay butterflies
> be careful of
> pine needle points
> in this gusty wind.'

When Mother saw Mr Tiffany Jones on the road she always stopped and asked, 'How is your wife?'

'Getting on; getting on, I hope,' said Mr Tiffany Jones, but he did not sound at all hopeful; he sounded wistful. He seemed to like watching Belinda and Nona with Mother, though when he saw the way Nona hung on her arm, and heard Belinda's chatter, his face would grow more wistful than ever. 'I wish Gem could be with her mother like this,' he said one day. 'When she does see her, she treats her as a stranger.'

'But you take Gem to see her often?' said Mother.

'Well, no,' said Mr Tiffany Jones. 'Agnes, my sister, says it would be too distressing. You don't think so?' he added, looking at Mother's face.

'It is distressing for a little girl *not* to see her mother,' said Mother. 'But perhaps Mrs Tiffany Jones will be coming home soon.'

'I should like her to, but Agnes says it would be too difficult,' and he sighed.

'Difficult! With all those servants,' said Anne when he had walked on. 'If you ask me, Miss Tiffany Jones likes bossing that lovely house and doesn't want to give it up,' but, 'You are not to gossip about things you cannot know,' said Mother.

'We do know,' said Anne. 'Anyone can see it and she likes bossing Gem too. Why doesn't he tell her not to? "Agnes says . . . ! Agnes says . . . !"' mocked Anne.

'Don't, Anne,' said Mother. 'You mustn't criticize the poor man. He is driven half out of his senses with worry.'

Chapter 4

'I'm going to spring-clean the dolls' house from top to bottom,' said Nona one wintry afternoon when the children could not go out.

'It isn't spring,' said Belinda.

'I mean clean it thoroughly,' said Nona, and before Belinda could argue about anything else, Nona ran out of the playroom and upstairs to her own room. Because it was such a dark and dismal afternoon, she turned on the light; she forgot to draw the curtains.

In Japan, houses are more simple and empty than ours. Walls are usually paper screens called *shoji* that slide backwards and forwards to let in the light, or to make doors and windows. The floors are covered with matting and Japanese people do not often use chairs, but have cushions to sit on; they have a low table or two, and a warm charcoal stove or firebox sunk in the floor round which all the family gathers. In the chief room is a niche called a *tokonoma* which has one picture hanging in it – a picture on a scroll that is changed to match the season; in winter, snowflakes perhaps; in spring, perhaps blossom; in summer a peony or a spray of morning glory or a bird; in autumn maple leaves that have turned red or yellow. A Japanese garden is part of the house, with trees and stones, perhaps a stone lantern, perhaps a curved bridge over a stream; often the bridges are so curved that they make a half hoop or crescent moon.

Nona's dolls' house was a dolls' house like that – a Japanese dolls' house. Tom had made it for her and, 'It must be the only one in England,' she often said proudly. It was raised on a plinth and had a flight of steps leading up to it. The walls were wooden with paper lattices that, in the front of the house, opened out into a pair of windows, while at the back, they were miniature shoji. Tom had made the screens for the shoji slide in the smallest possible grooves so that when they slid back, the house could be open to the garden. The lattices were of narrow strips of stiff white paper that criss-crossed. There was only one room in the dolls' house, but a hall led off it, divided by sliding screens of pale green paper. Japanese people call a hall the 'shoes-off' place, and Miss Happiness and Miss Flower kept their tiny clogs there. The floor was covered with matting – it was really a straw luncheon mat. There was a cupboard that was really a roll-top pencil box standing on its side: being a Japanese pencil box, a mountain – Fumi-Yama – was painted on its rollers. In it, in the daytime, the dolls' bed quilts and pillows were kept, and on its top were dolls'-house-size books and tiny bowls and platters. There was a firebox, the size of a matchbox, in which a bulb under red paper made a warm glow, a low table on which was a teapot and tea bowls, and beside it cushions in red and blue. The lamp was a cotton reel with a bulb fixed in its hole, and a painted paper shade; and the dolls had a dolls'-house television set. At the end of the room was the dolls'-house tokonoma, painted in pale green, with a polished black wood floor, and in it Nona always kept a scroll, a three-inch-long slip of paper with a shaved match each end to weight it. On this winter day, the scroll picture was of snowflakes and bamboos painted on brown paper. In a tiny yellow vase Nona arranged green pine needles and a single winter jasmine flower.

The dolls'-house garden lay behind the house; it had a looking-glass stream bridged with a half-moon wooden bridge that Tom had carved; there was a stone lantern too, that Nona had modelled in clay and fired in the school kiln; being up to date, the lantern was fitted with an electric bulb and could be switched on with the house lamp. Best of all, the garden had miniature trees, real ones, growing in the earth, a nine-inch-high cedar and an even smaller willow tree; they had been given to Nona by Mr Twilfit when the dolls'-house garden was made. The Christmas present she had liked best were some real miniature irises – not three inches high. 'They will flower in the summer,' said Nona.

Now she was arranging and dusting the house as she loved to do, and the dolls were helping her. Miss Happiness had an apron over her kimono, a handkerchief tied over her black hair; Nona had given her a duster the size of a postage stamp. In the garden Miss Flower was looking after Little Peach. Tom had made him a swing that hung from a branch of the cedar tree. Little Peach sat in it and every now and then, Nona gave it a gentle tap; it looked as if Miss Flower were really swinging him.

Nona was so busy playing that she never thought of looking up, of glancing across the way; if she had, she would have seen a small pale face pressed against the glass, fair hair falling each side of it – a book forgotten on the sill; someone was watching every move she made.

Perhaps you have been to the theatre and seen a stage lighted up; when the audience sits in darkness, the stage seems to come close, everything on it shows clearly. Gem's sitting room was in darkness and from it, that dark winter afternoon,

Nona's windowsill, the dolls' house and its garden seemed lighted liked a stage. You must remember how close the houses were. The ilex branches came a little across, but it was possible to look through the leaves.

Miss Flower looked across and saw Gem. In her silent, doll way she told Miss Happiness, 'Honourable little Miss Next Door is watching us.' Miss Happiness looked too, but Nona never even glanced across the way.

Gem stayed there until Matson came in, switching on the light, when she jumped and picked up the book she had forgotten and pretended she was learning her French verbs.

You may wonder why, if Gem watched Nona so

carefully, she always looked away when she met her or Belinda in the street and why she never smiled. I am afraid there was a reason.

Every Tuesday and Thursday afternoon, Belinda's class at school went to the Park to play netball, and when they were coming back, at four o'clock, they met Gem going to her dancing lesson. They walked two and two down the road, fourteen little girls, all fourteen of them dressed alike, in dark blue coats and berets, blue and yellow striped mufflers; this uniform made Gem seem more than ever conspicuous; she looked such a dressed-up little girl in her velvet coat, white fur cap and muff, white boots. Belinda and the others had short hair or plaits or ponytails; Gem's hair flowed down her back,

and always beside her walked Matson, carrying her shoes, her dressing case and a shawl.

'That's her Nanny,' Belinda told the girls at school. She had told them many things about Gem, in fact they knew all about her, and each time Gem passed, fourteen pairs of eyes looked her up and down, and there were fourteen sniggers. Presently there began to be little flipped remarks, not loud enough for the mistress at the back to hear, but quite loud enough for Gem:

'Here comes the snow queen.'
'Here comes the ballerina.'
'Don't catch cold, will you dear?'
'Nanny! Nanny! where's my handkerchief?'

Sometimes the mistress in charge of them was Mademoiselle and she would greet Gem in French so that Gem had to answer her, and 'Swank pot!' hissed the girls, or 'Parlez-vous français, s'il vous plaît.'

One of the girls had a rhyme:

'Gem T.J. tall and slender,
She's got legs like a crooked fender.'

Which was quite untrue; Gem's legs were perfectly straight. The only sign she gave that she had heard was that, as she walked past them with that stony face, she walked faster, while white patches came round her nostrils and she seemed to breathe quickly through them, her lips held tightly together. If Mademoiselle were there she would hurry even more.

Belinda thought it funny until she told about it at home. She told it shaking with laughter but, 'Belinda. Belinda. Belinda,' said Mother.

'You set them all on,' said Anne; 'I have a good mind to report you.'

'Fourteen against one,' said Tom. 'You little rotters.'

'It must have felt like whips,' said Nona.

Belinda felt ashamed, so much so that she began to whistle very loudly.

'No wonder Gem hates us,' said Nona.

'Well, I hate her,' said Belinda, but it is odd; when you have done something that is unfair to someone, you cannot get them out of your mind, and 'I do *wish* I could go next door,' said Belinda.

There were ways and ways of being disobedient and I think Belinda knew them all. 'You are not to go next door,' Mother had said but, 'If I am in the ilex tree,' said Belinda, 'how can I be next door?'

'You can't get up into the ilex tree,' said Nona. 'It's too high. Besides, the ilex tree is Tom's.'

The children all had their private and particular places in the garden where it was understood no other child trespassed. Anne had had the old white bench half hidden under the apple trees; now Nona had inherited it from her and often took Miss Happiness, Miss Flower and Little Peach there for secret picnics. Belinda had a cave at the back of the woodshed; Tom had the ilex. For two years running he and his friends, Stephen and Ronnie, had built a Swiss Family Robinson house up in the branches. None of the others had seen it, not even

Belinda. Though Belinda very often took no notice of Mother or even of Father, she always did what Tom told her, and 'You keep OUT,' Tom had said, and Belinda kept out. 'But that was last year,' she said now.

There came a half-holiday at the beginning of February, one of those still, sunny February days that seem as if spring had come. The snow had melted, there were snowdrops in the garden beds, and a bee buzzed round the catkins. Belinda was in the garden quite alone.

Father was, of course, at his office; Mother had taken Anne and Nona shopping, but Belinda had not wanted to go. 'Very well, you may stay here with Tom,' Mother had said.

Tom was in the garage, where he had his carpenter's bench. He was clever at making things; it was he who had made the Japanese dolls' house for Nona, and now he was making an oak bookshelf for Mother's birthday. He was trying to get it finished and was very busy. On the Tiffany Joneses' side of the hedge all was quiet too. They were all out. Mr Tiffany Jones was usually out all day, and Gem had gone riding. Belinda had watched her being put up on the white pony by the riding master; then they had trotted away. Matson, in her grey coat, had gone off in the direction of the shops. Presently Selwyn, looking unfamiliar in a greatcoat, had followed her. Miss Tiffany Jones had been driven away in the Rolls-Royce. 'Phantom Silver Cloud II,' murmured Belinda. She could hear television sounding from the maids' sitting room on the other side of the House Next Door. That meant Cook and Eileen were watching it. The gardener was in the potting shed; there was no one to watch Belinda or hear her, and – NOW, she thought, NOW.

'Tom, are you going to use the ilex house this year?'

Tom was busily planing a board and at first he could not hear her. She had to wait until he stopped to rest.

'This year are you going to use the ilex house?' she asked again.

'The ilex house?' asked Tom, as if he had never heard of it.

'The ilex house, up in the ilex, that you made with Stephen and Ronnie.'

'Oh that!' said Tom, and he asked, 'What do you think we are? Kids?'

That was what Belinda wanted to hear and her face beamed as she asked, 'Then can I have it? Can I?'

'If you like,' said Tom indifferently, and went back to his planing.

Belinda ran pell-mell off to the ilex, but Nona was quite right; when she stood close under it, the lowest branch was high out of her reach, while the house was higher up still. Looking up she could see planks, ropes, a ladder going up into the higher branches, a chair, a saucepan; it looked exciting, but how was it reached? She went back to Tom.

Once more she had to wait until he broke off from his planing. 'Tom, how did you get up?'

'Up where?'

'Up into the ilex.'

'We made a rope ladder,' said Tom, feeling down the board to see if it were smooth.

'I saw a ladder up there . . .'

'A *rope* ladder.'

'Where – is it?'

'Lashed to the first branch. We kept it rolled up there; that's how we stopped anybody getting up.'

'But how did *you* get up? To . . . to unroll it?' in her earnestness Belinda stammered.

'One of us got on the other chap's shoulders.'

'I haven't a chap,' said Belinda. 'Could I get on your shoulders? Would you let me? Oh Tom, will you come?'

'Sometime I will,' said Tom. 'Not now. I'm busy.'

'But I want it *now*. Please, dear darling Tom.'

'I'm not your dear darling Tom,' said Tom. 'You kicked me at breakfast this morning. Look,' and he showed a blue bruise on his shin.

Belinda had kicked him under the table because he had laughed at her. She was sorry now – Belinda was often sorry for things she did – but it was too late. He had already gone back to his planing. 'Hop it,' said Tom, and Belinda had to hop it.

The garden steps were too heavy for her to carry, as was the garden table, and if she had dragged it to the tree it would have left telltale marks on the grass. The garden chairs were flimsy and not high enough. Then what . . . ? Belinda looked round the garden and saw where Father, as soon as the snow had cleared, had begun hoeing the ground between the wallflowers in the long bed, raking the old dead leaves off. His wheelbarrow, half full of leaves, stood on the path, a big, heavy, wooden wheelbarrow.

Belinda emptied the leaves on the path; it was a struggle because the barrow was almost too heavy for her to tip and get upright again, but at last she was able to wheel it round the edge of the lawn until it stood under the ilex. The barrow was steady and firm; it needed to be that because in it Belinda began to build a tower. The barrow was just wide enough to hold a kitchen chair, a wooden one without arms. Then she found a box in the tool shed, an oblong wooden one that had once held sherry bottles; she stood it on the chair and on top of it put a big flowerpot, upside down. Then she climbed into the barrow and up on to the chair. The box left only a narrowest edge of chair seat around it, almost too narrow to stand on, but Belinda steadied herself against the ilex trunk, and managed to fit a foot each side of the box. Then, with a huge stretch, she got one foot on the box itself. It wobbled a little as she stood on it and she quickly levered herself further up against the ilex trunk and brought her other foot up to balance a foot each side of the flowerpot. Now she could reach the branch with her hand and could see a tied-up bundle of rope that must be the rope ladder, but she needed to be higher to untie it. Holding on to the branch with one hand, she stepped cautiously right up on the flowerpot. It was not very safe as she had to stand on one foot – there was no room for the other – but, feeling with her toe, she found a small hollow in the bole of the tree in which she could rest her second foot. Now she could almost stand square with her chest against the branch and she could use both hands to untie the ladder. That was hard work;

Tom's knots were undone and she was struggling with the others when, pulling on the obstinate rope, she jerked. It was a small jerk but it was enough! The flowerpot skidded away from her foot, the box shot sideways and the chair over-balanced and, crash, Belinda, flowerpot, box and chair toppled out of the wheelbarrow.

The chair and the box landed with a thwack, Belinda fell on her head, hitting her eye on the wooden wheelbarrow wheel, and the flowerpot bounced and caught her on the mouth.

For a moment tree, houses, sky seemed whirling round in front of her. She had a stinging pain in her eye, a hot wetness in her mouth, worse pain in her arm, and a burning in one of her knees.

'Ouch!' said Belinda. 'Ouch!' The pain was so bad that it made her feel sick, but she sat up on the grass while blood ran down her anorak jacket. Exploring with her tongue, she felt something in her mouth and spat; with the blood she spat out came something small and hard and white. It lay on the path and with her good eye she peered down at it. It was a tooth. 'Gosh!' said Belinda in awe. There was a rent in the knee of her trousers and through it showed a graze, dark red with swelling coming up around it. The sleeve of her anorak was ripped too, and her elbow hurt. Belinda was only just eight; she could not help two tears squeezing out of her eyes and she sniffled.

She spat out more blood, then slowly, painfully picked herself off the grass. She had thought she must go to Tom, but though the graze stung her and her elbow hurt, nothing seemed to be broken. The tree and the houses were steady again; from the ilex branch the ladder dangled, one side half-free, and, I had nearly done it — nearly, thought Belinda.

She had no handkerchief, 'as usual', Tom would have said, but she went round to the kitchen, hobbling because of her knee. Mrs Bodger had put some dusters on the windowsill to dry and Belinda took one to staunch her bleeding mouth. When she put her hand up to her eye, the hand came away red; she looked in the mirror Mrs Bodger kept over the sink, but though the eye was closing up, puffed and purple looking, the cut was more like a slit and not deep enough to bleed.

'Ouch! Ouch!' said Belinda, looking at it. Her lip was swelling too, and there was a dark gap where the tooth had been. It was altogether a piteous looking face that gazed back at her from the mirror — wait till Mother sees my trousers and anorak, thought Belinda.

The thought of Mother made Belinda cry a little more. What will she say? what will she? she thought, but it was no use thinking about it now. If you are obstinate you have also to be brave, and Belinda had a drink of water to help her stop crying and limped back to the ilex tree. She put the chair back in the barrow, the box on the chair, the flowerpot on the box, then painfully and much more carefully climbed up her tower again. She was not as agile now, and the pain made her more clumsy; she fell twice more. Once the box gave way, but she managed to hold to the branch and drop gently on to the grass, missing the path. Once she and the tower fell right down, but this time she was wary and managed to fall on her back. It made her mouth bleed again, which hurt, and her sleeve was ripped even more, but at last the ladder hung free from the branch, she was able to climb down and, 'After this, if I stand on the box – only the box – I can reach the ladder *easily*,' said Belinda. Yes, she could get up the ilex without Tom and, though it hurt to move her lip or eye, Belinda smiled.

She hid the box, put the chair back in the kitchen, the flowerpot back in the shed, and wheeled the barrow to where it had been left by the wallflower bed, and filled it with the leaves again as well as she could. Then painfully she straightened herself up.

Belinda was triumphant, but she was very sore and there was no sign of Mother, Anne and Nona coming in. It would be a long time before Father came back from the office and, I need a grown-up, thought Belinda. Tom was not grown-up, besides he would be cross with her. School was closed; Mrs Bodger lived at the other end of town but, 'I believe,' Belinda said to herself, 'I believe I shall go and see Mr Twilfit. He's so kind to Nona, perhaps he will be kind to me.'

She limped to the gate; her knee was beginning to stiffen up and hurt hideously, but she went on, out into the road. Then, as she turned to go down towards the shops, she found herself face to face with Miss Tiffany Jones.

Miss Tiffany Jones had just got out of the Rolls-Royce; the chauffeur, his arms full of parcels, was handing her a bunch of roses – 'Roses in February!' said Anne afterwards – but at the sight of Belinda the roses were left almost midair and, 'Good gracious!' said Miss Tiffany Jones. 'Good *gracious*!' She looked at Belinda's face, swollen and marked with tears and blood, at her puffed lip and closed-up eye; her torn anorak and trousers stained with grass and blood. '*Good gracious!*' said Miss Tiffany Jones again.

'It's the little girl from next door, Miss,' said the chauffeur.

'I know that,' snapped Miss Tiffany Jones.

'She seems to be hurt, Miss. Shouldn't we . . .' but Miss Tiffany Jones cut him short.

'You have been fighting,' she said to Belinda.

Belinda was offended. She was eight years old, and knew perfectly well that girls should not fight. 'Not with fists,' Tom had taught her; 'or kicking.' Belinda pulled people's hair – sometimes; she had been known to pinch, 'and scratch', Tom would have said; a year ago she might have kicked a table; she had kicked Tom that morning, but she would not have been in a fight that hurt people like this.

'Just playing,' said Belinda.

'Playing!' said Miss Tiffany Jones. 'Well, I certainly hope you confine that kind of playing to your own garden.'

'We will see that she does.' It was Mother's voice;

she, Anne and Nona had come up behind them, and in a moment Belinda was sobbing against Mother's coat. A cool handkerchief was in her hand and Mother's cool, careful fingers were examining the cut eye and the swollen lip, while Anne tenderly looked at the grazed knee. Nor did Mother say one word about Belinda's clothes. She merely said, 'Good afternoon, Miss Tiffany Jones.'

'I advise you to get your doctor,' said Miss Tiffany Jones; her voice sounded as if she were speaking to Mother twenty yards off instead of being just beside her. 'That cut looks dirty to me; you should certainly get the doctor.'

'I think I can deal with it,' said Mother quietly. 'Come, Anne and Nona,' and she led Belinda indoors. Soon Belinda was tucked up in bed, her cuts washed and dressed, her eye covered with ointment. Anne brought her a special supper on a tray; a bowl of soup, a roll of crusty bread, a private pat of butter, a plate of orange jelly, all laid on a pretty green cloth with a little vase of snowdrops. Belinda, leaning back on her pillows, felt a heroine.

Chapter 5

Sunday, Monday, Tuesday, Wednesday went by before Belinda could climb the ilex tree again. 'Days and days,' sighed Belinda. She was too sore and stiff to do more than hobble. Though her lip was better, her eye was so purple and swollen that Mother kept her back from school. She seemed, too, a little suspicious of what Belinda had been doing when she hurt herself and would not let her out of her sight. Mother had never once asked what happened to Belinda when she hurt herself so badly, though all the others had said, 'What were you *doing*?'

'I fell over the wheelbarrow,' said Belinda, which was true. She, the chair, the box and the flowerpot had fallen over the side.

'*Over* the wheelbarrow? How could you?'

'I did,' said Belinda.

'But how did you hurt yourself like that?' said

Anne, and Tom shrugged and said, 'Très rum.' Nona was wiser. 'I know what you were doing,' she said. 'Trying to reach the ilex branch.'

Mother asked no questions, but when Belinda was better Mother looked at her closely and said, 'Belinda, if I were you, I should try to put the Tiffany Joneses right out of your head.'

'Yes, Mother,' said Belinda, but how could she do that when the Tiffany Joneses were next door?

Then came another half-holiday, a Thursday, when Nona had a friend, Melly Ashton, to tea. Mrs Ashton brought Melly and was to have tea in the drawing room with Mother while the children had theirs in the playroom. Melly and Nona were there now, making a set of clothes for Peach Boy. Belinda knew what they were doing but as it was supposed to be a surprise, she had to keep out of the way. Anne and Tom were out; there was nothing for Belinda to do, and 'I believe,' said Belinda, 'even if I am still stiff and can only see out of one eye, I believe I will go up the ilex tree.'

As she let herself quietly out of the garden door,

she could hear Mother's and Mrs Ashton's voices in the drawing room, Nona and Melly laughing in the playroom. Belinda quietly shut the door, went round to the tree, and – though it hurt her leg – pulled the box out of the bushes. She got up on it and, holding on to the rope, stretched her foot up to the lowest rung of Tom's ladder. It could just reach and though she said 'Ouch!' when her weight came on her wrenched shoulder, she pulled herself up by her hands, then went up rung by rung until she reached the first branch. After that it was easy. She could climb from one branch to another until she came to the platform the boys had built for the floor of their house. It was not large; there was just room enough for a chair, two stools made of logs sawn off so that they stood levelly, and a rusty spirit stove. Then did they cook up here? Belinda wondered in admiration. It seemed they had; a packing-case cupboard was nailed to the tree and in it was what looked like a packet of dried-up sausages, a few old potatoes and a loaf, green with mould. Belinda threw them down the tree. There was also a spoon, a bottle opener, a plastic cup and a notebook in the cupboard. Belinda tried to read the notebook, but it was so soaked that the pages had stuck together and the ink had run. From the platform a ladder led up to the branches above, on which she could see three doormats tied. Were those their bedrooms, she wondered. The ladder, she could see now, was only a bit of a ladder, perhaps a cherry ladder that had broken off short, or Tom had sawn it, but it was high enough to reach the bedroom branches – about six feet long.

Now that she had seen it at last, Belinda did not think the house so very exciting; of course, it had been deserted long ago, but even then, thought Belinda. What did excite her was that from where the platform had been built against the ilex trunk, a pair of branches went across the hedge so far that they almost touched the fire escape to Gem's sitting room window. The lower branch was big, ending in a fork with a spread of dark green leaves; the upper branch was thin and leafy so that it made what Belinda called a roof over the lower one. I could sit on the big one, and wriggle to the fork, thought Belinda, and nobody would see me. Belinda never waited; in a second she had lowered herself from the platform to sit astride a branch; then she began to work herself forward.

It was perilous; the hedge, with the garden path on the Fells' side, and one of the Tiffany Joneses' new paved paths on the side of the House Next Door, was below her, the paths at least fourteen feet below, but it never occurred to Belinda to look down, and quite happily she worked her way along the branch, her hands holding it, her legs dangling. She was holding her breath too, with excitement, and her cheeks were crimson. Every now and then the big branch had small side ones, so that she had to slide her leg over them.

Now – though almost hidden by the ilex leaves – she was really close to Gem's sitting room window with the rose creeper round it; she could see right into the beautiful room with its desk and small white piano, the pale walls and flowered rugs; she could see the big dolls' house, dolls' beds and dolls' furniture; there were pictures, and the bookcases were filled with – dozens of books – thought Belinda. If she turned her head and bent sideways, she could

see into the bedroom too, with its pale blue four-poster bed, the dressing table that matched it and on which were small-sized silver brushes and combs and clothes brushes. A little armchair covered in rosy chintz had a dress laid on it ready for Gem to change into, a velvet dress with a ruffle round the neck. A book was thrown down by the bed.

We're not allowed to throw books down like that, thought Belinda virtuously, but on the other hand, Gem's shoes were not left all anyhow as Belinda's often were, but set neatly side by side . . . but Matson did that, I expect, thought Belinda.

Both rooms were more beautiful than any Belinda had seen but suddenly she was not looking at the rooms; she had seen something else. She looked, blinked, looked again, then quickly, far more quickly than she had come forwards, she wriggled backwards along the branch to the platform, where she turned herself round and, forgetting all about soreness and stiffness, almost tumbled down the branches. When she reached the ladder, she swung herself down it, dropped and landed on the grass and, not stopping to hide the box, ran limping and hopping into the house, where she burst into the playroom. 'What do you think?' panted Belinda, only she was so out of breath that the words all rang together; 'Whaddya think?'

Nona and Melly looked up in astonishment – Melly had hastily hidden their work under her dress. They looked astonished as, 'Whaddya think?' panted Belinda.

They did not know what to think, because they could not understand her. They had to wait until Belinda recovered her breath. 'Nona, Melly, what do you think?' Now the words were a little clearer. 'What *do* you think? She – Gem – *she* has a Japanese doll.'

Miss Happiness and Miss Flower were kneeling close beside Nona on their red and blue cushions while Peach Boy had a cotton reel as a stool; they too heard Belinda's announcement and, 'Then the Honourable Gentleman didn't only bring the lantern,' said Miss Happiness, and Miss Flower said, 'Another new person has come to live at the

House Next Door!' Together they softly whispered, *'Aisatsu suru,'* which is the Japanese for 'Welcome'.

Three people were on the big branch of the ilex tree; Nona behind Belinda, Melly behind Nona. They had both been frightened to leave the platform and go out along the branch; in fact Melly had had to shut her eyes and wriggle blindly forward holding on to Nona, but Belinda encouraged them in whispers, and now they were all far out on it, looking over one another's shoulders into Gem's sitting room and, 'There! I told you . . . look!' whispered Belinda. 'Look on Gem's windowsill.'

Nona and Melly looked in and, 'She *is* a Japanese doll,' said Nona, marvelling.

The doll was little, perhaps three inches high. 'Almost as small as Little Peach,' whispered Belinda, but she was unmistakably Japanese. She seemed to be made of the same plaster as the others, and perhaps had the same rag body, with a plaster face and little plaster hands and feet. Her feet were bare and, as if she were not much more than a baby, her legs were curved to sit down. 'Like Peach Boy's,' said Belinda. Her eyes were black glass, and she too had little painted eyebrows; her mouth was painted in red and looked like a half open rosebud. Her hair was black with a fringe, but she had a topknot wreathed with white blossom and pinned with a tiny silver pin. She was dressed in a pale blue kimono, the colour of a pale blue winter sky, patterned with sprays of white flowers, and her sash was pink.

'Look at her hair! Her topknot with the blossom!' whispered Melly.

'Look at her kimono, that's plum blossom on it,' whispered Nona.

'She looks like a girl Little Peach – Peach Blossom,' said Belinda. 'Only she's not peach, she's plum. Little Plum! That's her name.' In her excitement Belinda raised her voice. 'We will call her Little Plum.'

Nona hushed her, then objected, 'You can't give

a name to somebody else's doll.'

Belinda's eyes grew bright and determined. 'She is Little Plum,' said Belinda in a very loud whisper.

I wish I could go over and touch her, thought Belinda. I wish the big branch stretched that far. I wish our dolls could play with Little Plum. I wish, oh how I wish, thought Belinda, that I could go next door.

On the way back from school next afternoon, Nona and Belinda met Miss Tiffany Jones, and, to their surprise, she stopped them. Then she looked them over in her condescending way. They were certainly very different, in fact you could not imagine two more different girls. Nona – in her dark blue coat and beret – was neat, her striped school muffler was wound round her throat, the two ends crossed tidily on her back and held by a belt. Her long socks were straight, her shoes clean and she had on her gloves. Belinda had been in a hurry when she put on her things to go home: her beret was crooked, her coat buttoned wrongly, her muffler dangling anyhow. Her socks were falling down and her shoes were muddied where she had carefully stepped in all the puddles. 'Well, I like puddles,' said Belinda.

As Miss Tiffany Jones's eyes came to Belinda, her eyebrows went up, and her mouth turned down. Then she turned back to Nona. 'You seem a nice quiet child,' she said.

'Thank you,' said Nona. She did not know what else to say. She could not really believe she was talking to Miss Tiffany Jones.

'What's your name?'

'I am Nona. This is Belinda.' Nona tried to bring Belinda in, but Miss Tiffany Jones ignored her.

'You are . . . how old?'

'Nine,' said Nona. 'Belinda is eight.'

'Gem is nine too,' said Miss Tiffany Jones; 'my brother wants her to make friends with you and . . . yes, I should like her to have a nicely mannered little friend. I will write your mother a note.'

'She isn't my mother,' said Nona. 'She's my aunt.'

'Your aunt, to ask if you may come to tea.'

'*And* Belinda?' asked Nona.

Miss Tiffany Jones's gaze came back to Belinda; once more it went over the crooked beret, the wrong buttons, the trailing muffler, wrinkled socks and muddy shoes. 'Belinda?' she repeated; 'I'm afraid not Belinda; she is impossibly rough. I'm afraid I couldn't allow Gem to play with her.'

Belinda's face went as scarlet as if it had been slapped. She had to bite her lip to keep it from shaking, and she scuffed the pavement with the toe of her shoe. Colour came into Nona's face too, a bright pink spot on each cheek. Her head went up and she said, 'Thank you, but I don't go out to tea without Belinda.' She took Belinda's hand, and they walked away up the road. When they got into their own garden and the gate was shut, Belinda said through clenched teeth, 'I hate . . . I hate *all* Tiffany Joneses.'

Nona and Melly refused to go up the ilex tree again; indeed the children had had great difficulty in getting down it, but Belinda went up every day. 'Because I'm sorry for Little Plum,' she said.

Belinda, as you may have guessed, was not fond

of dolls. She liked ponies, boats, balls, roller skates, helping Tom with his carpentry. She was glad to let Nona – and Miss Happiness and Miss Flower, of course – look after Peach Boy; then why should she suddenly have such an interest in a little doll – and one that did not even belong to her.

'Gem doesn't play with her,' she told Nona.

'I expect she thinks she is an ornament,' said Nona.

'A doll an ornament!' Miss Happiness and Miss Flower were shocked but, 'I have seen Matson dust her,' said Nona.

'Dolls wouldn't need to be dusted if they were played with!' said Miss Happiness, and Miss Flower wished that her plaster neck would have let her shake her head in dismay. Nothing is worse for a doll than not to be played with. Perhaps Belinda caught their serious thoughts. '*Why* doesn't Gem play with her?' she asked.

Perhaps she doesn't know how,' said Nona.

'H'm!' said Belinda. She was silent a moment and then she said, 'It would be fun to teach her.'

'Nona,' she asked a day or two later, 'could you make a little padded coat?'

'A tanzen?'

'Yes, like Miss Happiness's and Miss Flower's, only smaller. Poor Little Plum looks so cold.'

Miss Happiness and Miss Flower were charmed. They had not ceased to talk and wonder about the little doll over the way. 'Miss Belinda wants to make Little Plum warm. Little Miss has a heart of gold,' they said but, 'You are not teasing Gem *again*?' asked Nona.

Belinda opened her eyes wide so that they looked very innocent. 'How could I tease her?' she asked. 'How could I when I never see her – and she will never see me?' said Belinda, and chuckled. 'Please make a little tanzen,' she begged.

In a day or two the coat was made; it was short, of scarlet silk wadded with cotton wool, with scarlet cords to tie it. Nona had learned the shape of a tanzen from the books Mr Twilfit had lent her. Nona was getting very clever with her fingers. 'Really, I think you sew better than Anne,' said Mother. To go with the coat was a pair of tabi, so small that they fitted the top of Nona's little finger. They too were soft and warm, 'and they should just fit,' she said. Then she, who hardly ever asked questions, did ask one. 'Belinda,' asked Nona; 'how will you get the socks and coat to Little Plum?'

That was the question.

'You could post them,' said Nona.

'Miss Tiffany Jones might open the parcel, or Matson,' said Belinda, and she said thoughtfully, 'Matson doesn't go near the windowsill after she has dusted, but Gem does now, two or three times a day. She stands there; I have seen her though she doesn't look at us.'

'She does,' said Miss Happiness, and Miss Flower could have said, 'Indeed she does. Little Miss often looks across at us,' but Belinda was too busy thinking to pay attention to the dolls. 'I must put the coat and socks on the windowsill,' she said.

'But how?' asked Nona.

'Somehow,' and Belinda went up the ilex tree to think.

She thought of getting Tom's fishing rod and dropping a parcel on Gem's windowsill, but how would she get the parcel off the hook? She was a good thrower but she could not be sure of throwing a parcel so that it would go in through the window or else lie on the window-ledge. It might drop down into the garden, the gardener finds it and takes it in to Miss Tiffany Jones.

'No, I must take it myself,' decided Belinda.

Even if she could have reached it, she could not climb up the rose; its stem was too slender, besides, it was prickly. She wondered if she could jump across on to the fire escape, but even holding on to the upper branch it would be difficult to jump off the fork and how could she jump back? She could perhaps have swung on the upper branch across on to the fire escape, then run down it to slip out through the garden . . . but I'm not allowed in the Next Door Garden, thought Belinda. She thought and brooded, and each time her eyes and her thoughts came back to the fire escape.

It was elaborate as everything belonging to the

Tiffany Joneses, a twisting spiral of iron with railings and a small landing on each floor; one of these landings was just by Gem's window. From the fork to that landing was not very far and suddenly . . . I believe I could make a bridge to it, thought Belinda. If I could slide, say a plank, or something, across until one end was on the fire escape, the other on the fork, then I could stand on the landing on one foot, put my other foot on that drainpipe; I could hold on to the fire escape railing with one hand and 'I believe,' said Belinda to herself, 'I believe I could just, just reach the window-ledge. If Matson had left the window open, I could put a hand inside.'

Most people, even children, would have thought of the danger of going across that space on a plank which would be narrower, not half as firm as the ilex branch. It would be high above the ground, and not protected or screened by other branches or leaves; most children would have thought of turning giddy, or of the plank wobbling, or falling, but Belinda did not give a single thought to any of these things. A plank, she was thinking, a plank. How can I get a plank, and if I get it, how can I get it up the ilex tree? It was then that her eye fell on the ladder.

There it was, already in the tree, the ladder Tom and the boys had brought up – one end resting on the platform, the other up the tree. It looked as if it might be the right length, not too long to manage, not too short to reach and, it's better than a plank, thought Belinda, if I can tilt it forward, tilt it so that it will come down slowly until it is resting flat on the branch . . . No sooner had Belinda thought these things than she jumped up to try.

She managed to ease the ladder forward a little so that she could stand behind it, and, I must push its top forward among the branches and see if I can bring it forward and down, thought Belinda and, standing with her feet apart and firmly planted, she gripped the ladder with both hands and pushed. The top came forward, then forward a little more. It caught on a small branch full of leaves and she had to shake it free; it scraped against big branches and she had to juggle it; then, suddenly, it became heavier, too heavy for Belinda; she tried to hold it but it came down with a rush that almost took her off her feet. Instinctively she let it go and, with a rending of leaves and branches, the ladder fell with such a thwack that it shook the whole tree. Belinda just missed being hit by the bottom of the ladder as it sprang up and bounced off the platform.

The spirit stove, saucepan, and chair went flying. It was a good thing no one was walking underneath, as Tom said afterwards. For Belinda, the thwack sounded as loud as a clap of thunder. She expected that heads would appear at all the Tiffany Joneses' windows; that on the Fells' side Mother and Tom, Anne and Nona would run out, calling, 'Goodness! What happened?' Belinda waited on the platform, making herself as flat as possible against the tree, shutting her eyes and holding her breath, but no one appeared, nobody called and soon the ilex leaves stopped shaking and she could dare to look. Luck was with her; the ladder had been caught by the smaller branches, and was lying just where she had wanted it to lie – along the big branch.

It was a little too sideways on but, with its weight

on the branch, it was easy for her to guide it into position and soon it was lying across the branch, one end resting on the fork. I can push it forward as I come forward myself, thought Belinda, push it right out until the far end lies on the fire escape. She was delighted. It's wider than a plank, she thought. Wider – nice and safe! The ladder was perhaps a foot wide, the drop to the path below was, as you know, all of fourteen feet, but Belinda did not think of that. She had her bridge.

When she had it in position, Belinda knew she must tie its near end firmly to the fork. She had that much sense. If I didn't it might slip sideways, she thought. She knew too she must be quick or somebody might see her. She cut a length of rope from the boys' store with Anne's Girl Guide knife that she was not supposed to touch. Little Plum's coat and socks were ready, pinned to a notice that Belinda had written; she had them in the pocket of her anorak. Now she sat down astride the branch behind the ladder, pushing it in front of her, and began to wriggle forward.

The ladder, polished and smooth with age, slid along the branch quite easily, more easily than Belinda – who had to keep stopping to slide a leg over a side branch. When she reached the fork, leaning forward she pushed the ladder on ahead. Will it be long enough, she asked, oh, will it? But it was just long enough. When one end rested on the fire escape, the other just lay on the fork. Belinda pulled her rope through the last rung, which was resting on the fork, and quickly lashed it until it was firm. When it was lashed, it did not wobble – very much, thought Belinda; but it wobbled a bit, and she breathed hard as she put first one leg, then the other, across the fork and levered herself forward until she was sitting on the ladder, a leg each side. It did not feel wide or safe; it felt thin and flimsy after the big branch, and Belinda almost went back but, 'It's only a little way,' she told herself.

It was certainly not as easy to wriggle forward along the ladder as it had been along the branch; her trousers kept on catching; she was afraid too that the end on the fire escape would tip up and she wished she could have lashed that end as well, but still she went forward, bit by bit, holding firmly with her hands, slipping them along in front of her. She did not once look down, which was as well, and in a minute her hand went out and caught the fire escape; then she was standing on the landing. With a beating heart she unpinned the notice and, facing the house wall, put her left foot on the drainpipe and, holding firmly to the railing with her right hand, she stretched out her left, being careful not to catch her sleeve on the rose thorns. The sitting room window was open a crack and, though this first time Belinda did not dare crane forward too far, she was able to stick the notice with the coat and socks through the crack. In two minutes more she had wriggled back along the ladder and was over the fork back in the ilex tree.

She could not turn round on the branch to unlash the rope; and she had first to go right back along it to the platform, where she turned round and wriggled forward again. Then she had to work herself backwards, pulling the ladder back along the branch, until it lay safely hidden among the leaves. Only then was she able to rest, sitting on the platform, but still breathing very hard and waiting for her heart to stop its pounding. She felt as if she had taken an hour but no, it was only minutes; nobody had come running, nobody had seen or heard, and Little Plum's coat, her socks, and the notice were safely on Gem's windowsill.

From the dolls' house, Miss Happiness and Miss Flower had seen the ilex shaking; they could just see the end of the ladder as it slid out to rest on the fire escape across the way and, 'Is it a bridge?' asked Miss Flower. If it were a bridge it looked exceedingly narrow and when they saw Belinda working her way to the end of it, their plaster seemed to creep with fear. Miss Flower especially felt as if she trembled. 'Little Miss is as brave as a dragon!' she said.

When Belinda reached the fire escape she was lost from their sight in ilex leaves but they saw her hand reach up to Gem's window. 'The new little doll has her coat and socks,' they told one another and, 'How pleased her little Miss will be with what our little Misses have done.' But of course, neither Miss Happiness nor Miss Flower knew what Belinda had printed in big letters on the notice: 'CAN'T YOU KEEP YOUR DOLL WORME?' Belinda had printed.

She had not been able to wait for Gem to come in because it was time for tea, but as soon as tea was over she slipped out again, ran to her ladder and climbed up. It was beginning to be dusk but she could see that her notice was gone. Little Plum was in her usual place on the sill opposite and she was not wearing the coat or socks. On the window-ledge outside was propped a notice, larger than Belinda's – Gem had used one of her expensive painting blocks. On it was printed in big letters: 'MIND YOUR OWN BUSINESS'. And underneath was written: 'And it's "warm", not "worme".' Next day Belinda found the scarlet jacket and the socks; they had been wrapped round a pebble and thrown over the hedge into the Fells' garden.

MIND YOUR
OWN BUSINESS
AND IT'S 'WARM' NOT 'WORME'

Chapter 6

'MIND YOUR OWN BUSINESS'. Nona would have minded hers at once but, 'Huh!' said Belinda, as if she were delighted, and next afternoon, 'Nona, haven't you another paper sunshade like the dolls' house one?' she asked.

Nona had found two sunshades in crackers at a party that Christmas. They matched the one that stood in the dolls' house 'shoes off' place and Nona had kept them carefully. Now reluctantly she took one out — it was pink with blossoms on it — and gave it to Belinda. 'I was keeping it in case . . .' she said, but Belinda was already writing. 'How do you spell "umbrella"?' she asked.

Gem almost caught Belinda that afternoon. Belinda had hardly got back to the platform and turned to draw back the ladder when Gem and Matson came up the garden path. Belinda was almost hidden by the top branch but not quite, and she froze as a rabbit does when it scents danger. 'Oh, don't look up! Don't!' prayed Belinda, and held her breath until Gem and Matson had passed safely into the house. Then she had to hurry and untie the ladder from the fork, but she tried so hard to be quick that her hands fumbled and she had only just time to draw back when Gem came into the sitting room. As fast as she could Belinda wriggled back to the platform and flattened herself against it and, 'What will Gem do when she sees the sunshade?' asked Belinda. She had put it on the windowsill with a message: 'We take our dolls OUT. Why don't you? If you're afraid of rane, here's an umbrella.' The sunshade was not an umbrella, but Miss Happiness and Miss Flower could use theirs in the rain because Nona had painted it on the outside with oil.

Belinda had not long to wait. In what seemed a minute the window opened wide and the sunshade was thrown out, thrown by Gem's hand, and hard. It was open, and like a little parachute, it caught

the wind and floated, eddying towards the Fells'
garden, and Belinda saw that it went so well because
it was weighted by a screwed-up paper. A message,
thought Belinda. It eddied over the Fells' garden,
coming lower and lower.

Belinda ached to go and catch it, but with Gem
at the window she had to stay where she was —
and as still as that frozen rabbit. Suppose I sneeze,
thought Belinda, and at once she wanted to sneeze.
Luckily Tom had taught her a trick of rubbing her
finger hard under her nose and she just managed
not to sneeze.

The sunshade came down, caught in a forsythia
bush in the Fells' border, but still Gem stayed
watching at the window, while Belinda grew colder
and colder; she could not feel her feet at all, her
hands ached with cold and her nose was running
but, she's trying to trap me, thought Belinda.
Nothing would have made her move.

It was growing dark; soon Mother would miss
her; people would be set to search: Tom, Anne,
Nona, presently Father; then Mother must find out

what she was doing. Belinda knew without telling that Mother would be very annoyed. She began to think she should have to move when the Tiffany Joneses' gate opened, and there was Gem's music master coming as he did every Monday, Wednesday and Friday. Belinda had forgotten it was Friday and, it must be half past four, she thought. At the same moment the lights in Gem's sitting room went on and Matson stood there in the doorway, telling Gem to come down. Gem had her lessons on the grand piano in the drawing room; she only used the little white piano for practising.

Because the window was shut, Belinda could not catch words, but she could hear their voices – Matson's expostulating, Gem's curt – and see their gestures. 'I won't come down,' Gem seemed to be saying. 'You must, Miss Gem,' Matson was answering and, 'I won't move,' said Gem. Matson must have gone to get Miss Tiffany Jones, for that large lady appeared in the doorway. At the sound of her loud voice Gem left the window quickly and, she doesn't want Miss Tiffany Jones to know, thought Belinda. At least Gem was not a sneak. Miss Tiffany Jones spoke so peremptorily, that slowly, reluctantly, Gem went out of the door. Belinda had almost moved when Gem suddenly whipped back again, ran to the window and took a hasty peep.

'Ha! ha! You thought you would catch me,' said Belinda under her breath and, cold, as she was – shivering, thought Belinda – she made herself stay quite still until she heard Gem's scales going up and down and was sure that it was safe to come down.

She was chilled to the bones but it was just light enough in the garden to find the sunshade parachute. She had to take it indoors before she could read the message, which was written in small clear writing; what it said was clear too: 'Trespassers will be prosecuted', Gem had written. 'If I find you in our garden, I shall call the POLICE.'

When they saw the pink sunshade thrown out of the window, Miss Happiness and Miss Flower were grieved. 'But why?' they asked. 'Why? We had hoped Little Plum would go out into the world and

perhaps come and visit us.' Something was going on that they did not understand, but it was certainly exciting. 'What will little Miss Belinda think of next?' they asked.

'Nona, can you make a Japanese dinner on a tray?'

'Yes, but you will have to buy a dolls'-house tea set,' said Nona.

'Buy it with my own money?'

'If you want a Japanese dinner,' said Nona.

Belinda had not told Nona how the jacket and socks had come back, the sunshade been thrown out, nor told her of Gem's messages, but Nona seemed to have a shrewd idea of what was happening. 'If I lend Miss Happiness's and Miss Flower's bowls and tea things, anything might happen to them,' she said.

'You can buy one of those painted metal tea-sets; Tom would file the handles off the cups to make the bowls. There is a pretty pink set in the window at Merrow's shop and they only cost nine pence.'

'Nine pence! That's heaps of money,' said Belinda. 'I can't spend nine pence on Gem.'

'Then you can't have a Japanese dinner.'

'And why a teapot for dinner?' Belinda was trying to argue, but Nona was firm.

'Japanese people seem to have tea with every-thing – green tea – I can make that with paint water.'

Belinda hated to spend her pocket money, but Gem's last message had been really rude and, 'I'll show her who's trespassing,' said Belinda.

Nona had never made anything prettier than that tray. She made it from the lid of an old pillbox, and painted it shiny black outside, scarlet inside for lacquer. She gummed the pink bowls on to it in case Belinda spilled them, and gummed the food on as well, but dolls are used to having dolls' house food fixed on with gum. There were notices the size of half your little finger-nail, to say what each bowl held: 'rice', said one – that was snipped-up white cotton; 'fish' – they were cardboard fish as small as ants, painted silver in a red sauce ('Japanese people are very fond of fish,' said Nona); 'vegetable' – ground up green parsley in another sauce; 'cake' – pink and white meringue sugar crumbs. There were chopsticks made from pine needles and, what was most wonderful of all, the tea was hot. Tom had filed the teapot handle off as well as the cup handles and bored two tiny holes, through which Nona threaded a loop of brown cotton and buttonhole-stitched it so that it looked like a wicker handle such as real Japanese teapots have. Belinda had taken the tea over in an old aspirin bottle, keeping it in her pocket so that it should not get cold. 'It was boiling when I put it in,' she told Nona.

Miss Happiness and Miss Flower hoped Gem, when she found the tray, would play with it. 'Pour out a bowl of tea,' Miss Happiness and Miss Flower tried to tell her when they saw her at the window. 'Make Little Plum use those chopsticks.' But again Miss Happiness and Miss Flower had not seen the message that had come with the tray: 'Why don't you give your poor starving doll some FOOD?'

Gem read it and next moment tray, food, bowls, saucers, teapot, chopsticks, everything had gone out of the window.

As soon as Gem was out of the way next day – gone for a walk in the Park with Matson – Belinda went up in the ilex tree to see how Gem had liked the dinner. She soon saw! Down below on the path was something scarlet, black and pink, a thrown-down tray, its food all scattered, while, on Gem's windowsill, close by the ledge, was a small china pot with a cover. By it was a notice printed: 'FOOD FOR YOU.' When Belinda had spied round to see both gardens were empty she went across to get it. Whatever can it be? thought Belinda.

When she was safely down again, she took the cover off the pot; inside was something that looked like dreadfully smelling, dreadfully coloured jam – covered by a piece of paper that said: 'My own recipe.' The recipe was written out in Gem's pretty handwriting:

'Vinegar
Mustard
Castor oil
Toadstools
Frogs' eggs
Crushed cockroach
Worms.'

At the bottom was written: 'Take it.'

'Good heavens gracious me!' said Belinda, her eyes round. After the first minute, she thought it was funny but when she showed it to Nona, Nona was not as sure. 'I don't like it,' said Nona.

'We're not meant to like it,' said Belinda.

'You're teasing Gem,' said Nona; 'don't go on.'

But Belinda said, 'We're not teasing now. We're fighting.'

The war had now been on for three weeks and, 'Little Plum needs a bed,' said Belinda. 'Nona, can you and Melly make her some quilts and pillows?'

Japanese people do not have bedsteads – only

those who copy Western habits. Most sleep on the floor on thick quilts piled one on top of the other, with more quilt coverings and a hard pillow for their heads. 'They used once to have wooden pillows,' said Nona, 'but all the same Japanese quilt beds are very comfortable. Miss Happiness and Miss Flower could have told you that. They each had sets of quilts, one all in blue, the other in pale pink. Peach Boy had a scarlet set but he usually slept in the pocket of Belinda's dressing gown, which was flung down on the end of her bed, or on the floor.

Nona chose some flowered stuff, palest blue, to match Little Plum's kimono, with a pattern of blossom, and made two quilts for Little Plum to lie on, wadded with cotton wool, a pillow with tassels at the corners and an overquilt, thinner but wadded too. It was the prettiest set she had made. 'I think Gem will like it,' she said.

'I believe, if the window was open, I could put Little Plum into the quilts,' said Belinda. 'I believe I could reach; if I don't put her into them, I'm sure Gem won't. Poor Little Plum!' said Belinda.

It is certainly tiring for a little doll to have to sit all the time. 'Never to lie down,' said Miss Flower. 'Never to be moved,' said Miss Happiness. They were pleased that now Little Plum could go to bed – but could she?

You may wonder, if Gem wanted Belinda – she was sure the trespasser was Belinda – to mind her own business, why she did not put Little Plum out of reach, or out of sight.

'Perhaps she likes the things we sent,' said Nona. Remember that Belinda had not told Nona how Gem had thrown the jacket and socks over the hedge; how she had cast out the sunshade and smashed the dinner tray and, 'I think Gem's pleased,' said Nona, but Belinda shook her head.

'She just wants to catch me,' said Belinda.

Belinda had to take Little Plum off Gem's windowsill to put her into the quilts.

'Where is she going?' cried Miss Happiness and Miss Flower as they saw a topknot and a flowery kimono in Belinda's hand up in the air: but, in a moment, Little Plum's legs were straightened and she was slid between covers much warmer and more silken soft than anything she had ever known: a pillow was tucked under her head and a minute later she was back on the

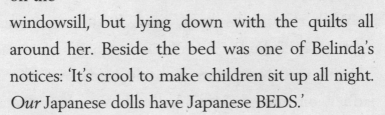

windowsill, but lying down with the quilts all around her. Beside the bed was one of Belinda's notices: 'It's crool to make children sit up all night. *Our* Japanese dolls have Japanese BEDS.'

Next day a paper bag was hanging from Gem's windowsill. When Belinda went over and got it, she found there was no message inside; no message was needed; in the bag were the pretty quilts and pillow snipped to bits.

Even Belinda was a little dismayed. She showed the bag to Nona and Nona could have cried. 'But why?' she asked. 'Why? It took me *hours* to sew those quilts,' and she said, touching the snippets,

'Belinda, what are you trying to do? Make Gem like Little Plum or make her hate you?'

'Make her like Little Plum, of course,' said Belinda.

'You would do it better without insulting messages,' said Nona.

'Are they insulting?' asked Belinda with great satisfaction.

'You know they are.'

'Well, she insults back,' and, 'Gem's a good fighter,' said Belinda.

Gem was. Next time Belinda went over the ladder, on one of Gem's ballet lesson days, the window was open wider than usual. Before Nona had seen the quilts snipped up, she had made Little Plum a cushion to match them, and Belinda had determined to sit Little Plum on it. She had written a notice: '*Our* dolls have coochons to sit on.' She was in a hurry because she only got back from school a few minutes before Gem was due in and she was perhaps not as careful as usual; as she reached up for Little Plum her hand knocked the window frame.

There was a blinding icy cold splash, something hit Belinda on the head and nearly sent her spinning off the drainpipe. How she kept her foot on it and clung to the fire-escape railing she did not know, because she was gasping for breath and spluttering; then she saw that the window was streaming with water while far below where she might have fallen was a small white plastic bucket, still rolling a little from its fall. It lay beside the cushion that had been knocked out of Belinda's hand, and 'Sh-she s-set a b-booby trap for me,' said Belinda through her chattering teeth.

It was a successful trap. How Gem had put the bucket up without Matson knowing, the children never knew; as the bucket was white and hidden a little in the rose creeper Belinda, in her hurry, had not seen it against the white house wall; nor had she noticed that the window was open wider than usual, and unfastened so that it swung at a touch. There had not been a great deal of water in the bucket – if there had been Gem could not have

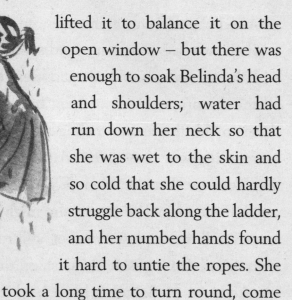

lifted it to balance it on the open window – but there was enough to soak Belinda's head and shoulders; water had run down her neck so that she was wet to the skin and so cold that she could hardly struggle back along the ladder, and her numbed hands found it hard to untie the ropes. She took a long time to turn round, come back for the ladder, draw it in, and climb down the ilex tree again. Fortunately Gem was late, but by the time Belinda got back to the house she was shivering from head to foot.

The first person she ran into was Mother. 'Belinda!' cried Mother. '*Belinda!* Where *have* you been?'

'Into a bucket of water,' said Belinda truthfully.

'But how . . . ?'

'It fell on me,' Belinda was just going to say, but Mother had seen how she was shivering and she wasted no more words. In a few minutes Belinda was in a hot bath. Mother was rubbing her hair dry with warm towels and had called to Nona to make a hot milk drink.

'She might have killed me,' Belinda whispered to Nona when she was dressed again in dry clothes and Nona had brought the milk, into which she had put some honey. 'I might have been dead!' Belinda sounded thrilled but Nona was remembering the snipped up quilts and, 'Belinda, give this up,' she begged.

'What! Now?' said Belinda. 'Let her win now? Wait . . .' said Belinda, and her eyes were bright blue over the top of the glass of milk. 'Wait and see what *I'm* going to do to *her*!'

When the bucket fell on Belinda, Miss Happiness and Miss Flower had been shocked, almost as shocked as Belinda herself. Japanese are courteous people and, 'Little Misses to do that to one another!' they said. They were not only shocked, they were worried about Little Plum, because some of the water had surely splashed on her. 'And Little Plum has no mother to put her into a hot bath,' said Miss Flower, 'to rub her hair dry.'

'No Miss Nona to make her a hot drink,' said Miss Happiness. They knew that Gem would not think of a little doll being cold, her plaster almost frozen, on the windowsill.

Miss Happiness and Miss Flower were beginning to understand that Little Plum was in the middle of some sort of quarrel, and they did not know what to wish for: that Belinda would stop climbing the ilex tree; that Gem could learn to play; 'That we should all be peaceful and happy together,' said Miss Happiness. The two little dolls were still talking it over that late afternoon when there came a sudden and determined shaking in the ilex tree.

Chapter 7

Gem walked out of the Tiffany Joneses' gate and in at the Fells'. Matson was not with her, nor Miss Berryman. She wore her velvet dress with the net ruffle and had only a coat put round her; no gloves or white boots, only bronze house shoes. Her head was bare and she had no shawl. She went to the front door and rang the bell. Mother came to answer it and, 'Why, Gem!' cried Mother.

'Will you please,' said Gem in a strange high tone – it was the first time Mother had heard

her speak – 'Will you please tell your child, Belinda, to give me back my doll?'

Mother opened the door wider and said, 'Come inside, out of the cold.'

When Gem was in and the door was shut Mother asked, 'Does your aunt, does Matson, know you are here?'

'No, they don't,' said Gem. 'But it doesn't matter. I have only come to get my doll.'

'Your doll?'

'Yes, my doll.' Gem spoke as if Mother was her enemy.

'But what makes you think she is here?'

'I know she is,' said Gem. 'That's why. Please give her back.'

'But how could she be?' asked Mother. 'How could a doll of yours be here?'

'I don't know how,' said Gem, 'but she is here. She was on my windowsill – a little Japanese doll – and she's gone.'

'A *Japanese* doll,' said Mother, and she asked, 'When did she go?'

'This afternoon.'

Mother suddenly looked at Gem in a different way. 'It wouldn't by any chance have something to do with a bucket of water?'

Gem's eyelids came down over her eyes like seals and she shut her lips.

'Come into the sitting room,' said Mother, and she called down the passage to the playroom, 'Belinda, come here. I want you.'

Belinda came. When she saw Gem, though she tried not to let her face show anything, she could not help a smile.

'Belinda, answer me truthfully. Have you got Gem's doll?'

'No, I haven't,' said Belinda, but Mother was not satisfied.

'Do you know who has?'

'No,' said Belinda, but Mother seemed to guess she might have said more.

'Do you know anything about her?'

'Of course I do,' said Belinda. 'We all do. Gem has a dear, sweet little Japanese doll called Little

Plum – such a pretty little doll with a topknot – and she takes no care of her. I'm not surprised to hear she's lost,' said Belinda.

Before Mother or Gem could say anything to that there were sounds from the garden next door; agitated sounds of, 'Gem! Miss Gem! Miss Gem, where have you got to? Gem, are you hiding? Miss Gem! Gem!'

'They have missed you,' said Mother, but Gem did not seem to have heard. She was glaring at Belinda, and Belinda glared back.

'I had better tell them where you are,' said Mother. 'Stay here, Belinda. We will sort this out when I come back.'

Gem and Belinda were left alone. Belinda was slightly afraid of Gem; she looked so fierce with her face set, her green eyes blazing. Belinda had never seen anyone in such a towering temper.

'How dare you take my doll?' said Gem.

'I didn't take her; I rescued her . . . for her own good,' said Belinda, who had heard her headmistress say that. 'You were cruel to her.'

'I was not,' said Gem.

'You were,' said Belinda.

'You took her. You're a thief.' Gem came one step nearer, Belinda instinctively took one back. 'Thief! Trespasser! Liar!'

'I'm not a liar.'

'You were telling lies to your mother just now.'

'I was not,' but Belinda's voice was uncertain. 'I was *not*. I haven't got your doll, see; I don't know who has her because nobody has her. She's by herself in a safe place. So bah!' said Belinda, as they said at school. 'So bah! Squish squash, flat on the floor.'

'*You'll* be flat on the floor.' Belinda backed away as Gem came closer, breathing in an alarming way through her nostrils. Her words came out through set lips. 'Thief!'

'Cruel!' Belinda retorted. 'Cruel beast.'

'Thief! Liar! Trespasser!'

'Beast! Beast! Beast!'

Then Gem sprang at Belinda and Belinda forgot all Tom's teaching, and hit out with both fists. She pulled Gem's hair. Gem screamed and hammered Belinda with her fists, and in a moment they were locked together, rolling, thumping, scratching and kicking, on the floor.

'Good gracious! Gracious! Help!'

'Miss Gem! Miss Gem!'

Miss Tiffany Jones and Matson were in the doorway. When they stood together they could not get in, and you could hardly see Mother behind them.

'Belinda! Belinda!' screamed Nona from under Matson's arm. She dodged under it, squeezed past Miss Tiffany Jones and jumped in to help Belinda but, '*Belinda!*' Mother had thundered in such a voice that Belinda let go of Gem. Matson, with surprising quickness, ran in, caught Gem and held her, while Nona pulled Belinda away.

Both children were panting. Belinda had a scratch right down her cheek, more scratches on her hands and her hair was tousled, while Gem's was hanging over her face. The beautiful velvet dress was torn, its net ruffle hanging down. Belinda stared at it aghast. One of Gem's high white silk socks was torn, her cheek was cut where it had hit a chair, and her face was beginning to swell.

Miss Tiffany Jones was silent now; she seemed too appalled to speak. Matson gave grunts of consternation and began dabbing at Gem's cheek with her handkerchief. Nona stroked Belinda's shoulder in silent sympathy. 'It wasn't meant for a fight,' said Nona, trying to explain. 'It was just that it turned into a fight.'

'A fight about what?' asked Miss Tiffany Jones faintly.

'About Little Plum,' said Nona.

'Little Plum? Little Plum? Who is Little Plum?'

As Miss Tiffany Jones said that Gem began to laugh.

'Belinda, go up to your room *at once*,' commanded

Mother. Belinda went, but Gem still went on laughing – it was a horrible high laughing that Nona did not like to hear. Matson picked up Gem's coat, wrapped it round her and took her away, still laughing.

'But . . . but it's nothing to laugh at,' said Miss Tiffany Jones in bewilderment.

Gem and Belinda were both in their rooms, Belinda because she was punished, Gem because she would not come out. Nona had seen how, in the garden, she had torn herself away from Matson and run into the house.

She must have run upstairs because when Nona went into her own room, she could hear knockings, and voices calling over the way, 'Miss Gem! Miss Gem! Open the door.' It seemed that Gem took not the faintest notice. Uneasy and unhappy, Nona watched and listened. Presently, Matson and Miss Tiffany Jones gave up and there was silence and, with a sigh, Nona turned away from her own window but, before she left it, she bent as she often did to look in the dolls' house. It always comforted her to see Miss Happiness and Miss Flower. She bent down, and stopped. She had caught sight of Miss Flower's pale blue bed, quilts and pillow, lying out on the matting. In the daytime? thought Nona, puzzled. I didn't put them there. She bent right down to look into the house properly, and there, on Miss Flower's blue pillow lay an unmistakable topknot. 'Little Plum!' cried Nona. 'Little Plum!'

The dolls had been astonished when Little Plum had suddenly appeared in their house; astonished, although, 'Of course she is very welcome,' they said courteously.

'But it seems strange,' Miss Flower could not help saying, 'that a guest should go straight to bed.'

'It was Miss Belinda's idea,' said Miss Happiness. 'If Miss Nona had been here, she would at least have let us offer her some tea.'

'That would have been more polite,' and Miss Flower could not help feeling that when things were not polite they were somehow wrong.

'We should have bowed to her and she to us,' and

then Miss Flower sank her voice. 'Is she a refugee?' she asked.

'I don't think so,' said Miss Happiness. 'Refugees are people who have run away or been driven out. I think Little Plum was brought here,' said Miss Happiness.

'Kidnapped?' asked Miss Flower in alarm. 'Would our Miss Belinda do that?'

'I hope not, but I think so,' said Miss Happiness.

Meanwhile Little Plum's topknot looked so comfortable on Miss Flower's pillow, she seemed so content lying there in the pale blue quilts, that it was as if she were saying, 'Let me lie here forever.' But Little Plum was still in the middle of a quarrel. Nona's face had filled with consternation and the next minute her hand had taken Little Plum out.

'You must give her back *at once*,' said Nona.

Belinda knew she was on losing ground. Nona's scandalized face and wrathful eyes made her feel uncomfortable.

'At once!' said Nona.

'Mother says I mustn't come out of my room,' said Belinda, but feebly.

'She would want you to come out for this. She has gone to Miss Tiffany Jones, to explain,' said Nona, but how could Mother explain that . . . Nona hated to say it but she had to . . . that Belinda had stolen Little Plum. 'Oh Belinda!' said Nona. 'How can you be so bad?'

'Gem was unkind to Little Plum.'

'She wasn't unkind – she was just not kind; but that doesn't matter. You must put Little Plum back where you found her – at once.'

'Then Gem will win,' said Belinda sulkily.

'She deserves to win,' said Nona, and like a policeman she put Little Plum into the pocket of Belinda's anorak, which she fetched from the cloakroom, and chivvied Belinda down the stairs. There she turned across the garden towards the gate, but Belinda stopped. 'I have to go up the ilex tree,' said Belinda.

'The ilex? To get up to Gem's window? But . . .

I thought you went up the fire escape; you can't reach from the ilex tree.'

'I can. Wait. You'll see.'

Slowly, sullenly, Belinda went up the tree. Nona stood at the bottom of the ladder, looking up, mystified as to what Belinda was doing, but when Belinda reached the big branch, she stopped. The light was on in Gem's sitting room and Belinda could see in. Gem was sitting at her desk, her face down on her arms, her shoulders shaking and, 'Nona,' Belinda whispered urgently, 'Nona, Gem's crying.'

'Crying? She was laughing.'

'She's crying now.' Belinda saw how Gem's shoulders shook, how great sobs shook all of her and, 'She's crying terribly,' whispered Belinda.

Nona climbed up the ladder on to the platform and looked in too. 'Oh Belinda, what have you done to her?' said Nona.

'Did I do that?' asked Belinda, startled. She was a rough, tough little girl but she had a tender heart and now, at the sight of Gem so hopelessly crying, a lump began to gather in her own throat and she had a miserable, guilty feeling.

'What can I do?' she whispered to Nona.

'I don't know how you got up to the window,' said Nona, 'but do as you did before. Then tap on it and give Little Plum to Gem.' Nona still thought Belinda would come down, slip across the two gardens and go up the fire escape. It had not occurred to her there was any other way to the House Next Door, and she turned to lead the way, climbing off the platform and from branch to branch down the tree, then down the rope ladder. At the foot of the ilex she stood and waited for Belinda, but Belinda did not come. Instead there were queer sounds up above and, 'What are you doing?' Nona called up.

'Getting the ladder ready,' said Belinda calmly.

'What ladder?' Then Nona saw the wooden ladder sliding into position, one end on the fire escape, the other on the fork. In a moment Belinda was lashing it firm. 'You're not . . . you're not going across *that*!' cried Nona in horror.

'Why not?' said Belinda. 'I often do.'

'No! No! Belinda, no!' Nona almost screamed, but Belinda was already astride the ladder, her legs dangling, her hands in front of her as she wriggled forward. Nona, looking up, saw the sickening drop from the ladder to the path and she could not look any more. She cowered against the ilex tree and hid her eyes.

That was why she did not see Mother come back from the House Next Door. Mother had met Tom outside the gate. Now, from the path, they saw Belinda. Mother stood still. Tom was just going to shout when Mother's hand came down on his shoulder. 'Hush! don't shout; don't move,' she said. 'If you make her look down she will fall.' All the colour had drained out of Mother's face, her eyes were wide with terror. As they stood there, Mr Tiffany Jones came walking up to the gate of the House Next Door. He had his hand on the latch to open it when from the Tiffany Joneses' garden came a piercing scream.

It was Matson. Thinking that perhaps Little Plum had been dropped in the garden, Matson had gone to look. 'Children beat me,' Matson had said to Selwyn. 'Gem didn't care at all about that doll, and now suddenly . . .' Matson was beating the bushes when she happened to look up. At her scream Mr Tiffany Jones looked up too. Then he flung open the gate and ran in. Miss Tiffany Jones, Selwyn, Cook, Eileen all rushed out of the house; the gardener threw down his broom and ran too, and all the while Matson pointed and screamed. In her room Gem lifted her head from her desk and listened, then came to the window to look.

Mother and Tom ran from their side of the garden; Nona stood, pressed back against the trunk of the ilex tree, and high above them all, halfway across the ladder, Belinda heard.

She heard and looked down. She saw faces staring up at her, the pointing hands and, as if their fear had come up to her, suddenly Belinda was afraid. She had never looked down before. Now, her feet below her, she saw the path; there was nothing each side of her but the empty air and she felt how narrow the ladder was, how her legs were dangling in nothing – and all at once she felt giddy and sick. Cold drops came out on her forehead, and the backs of her knees. Her hands felt damp. She swayed. Below, on the lawn, Miss Tiffany Jones fainted away.

By now Tom was past Nona, up the ilex tree and out along the branch. 'Hold on,' called Tom, 'I'm coming.' But, big boy that he was, when he reached the fork and the ladder Tom could not make himself get on it.

'Don't go, Tom. Don't go,' Nona whispered up frantically. She need not have said it. Tom could not make himself go. He lay along the branch and tried to reach Belinda, but he could not. 'Come back, Bel,' he said. 'Come back towards me.' But, 'I can't,' gasped Belinda, 'I can't.'

She who had gone across the ladder so many times could not move now; she could only sit and shut her eyes and cling with her hands.

'Don't look down. Don't,' came Mother's even voice, but Belinda could not look anywhere. Matson's noise had been joined by Cook and

Eileen, Selwyn had run in again to telephone the fire brigade, while a crowd began to gather in the road. A woman screamed louder than Matson. A whole tumult of sound was gathering, beating in Belinda's ears, when a voice spoke close beside her. 'Open your eyes,' it said, 'and look at me.'

It was such a quiet voice in the hubbub that it reached Belinda. She opened her eyes and there, on the fire escape, just in front of her, was Mr Tiffany Jones. His brief-case, his bowler and his beautiful great-coat were cast down on the landing, and he was holding the end of the ladder, speaking to her. 'Brave girl,' came that quiet voice. 'Look at me.' It was wise to keep on saying it.

Below, on the path, Selwyn and the maids had spread a blanket and were holding it to catch Belinda if she fell but, 'You won't fall,' said Mr Tiffany Jones steadily. 'Look straight at me. Now move your right hand forward.'

'I – can't,' said Belinda through stiff lips.

'You can.'

'I – can't,' and to everyone's horror, Belinda swayed again. 'I'm – I'm going to fall,' she said in a rush.

'Fall? With Gem looking?'

'Gem?' Belinda stiffened.

'Gem's watching you,' said Mr Tiffany Jones. 'Watching you from the window.'

Belinda looked up and there was Gem's face pressed against the glass, pressed tightly, looking at Belinda.

'Do you want her to think you're a coward?' came Mr Tiffany Jones's voice. 'Do you want her to laugh at you and think you're afraid?'

'I'm not afraid.' The words were jerked out of Belinda.

'Then move your right hand,' and suddenly Belinda was able to obey. 'Come forward an inch. Move your right hand . . . now your left. Come forward,' said Mr Tiffany Jones. 'Come or she'll think you are afraid.' His face was oddly pale and he too had wet drops on his forehead. Belinda could see them running down his cheeks but he was smiling at her and he still held her in his eyes. 'Your right hand forward. Now your left . . . come forward. That's right. You show Gem you're not a coward.'

A hush had fallen on the garden and the street as Belinda began to move. Mother stayed silent down below, Tom silent in the tree, Nona silent at its foot. Gem was silent at the window, her hands clutching the sill. Slowly, as Mr Tiffany Jones commanded her, Belinda moved along the ladder towards the fire escape. She had been perhaps only two feet out of Mr Tiffany Jones's reach, but it seemed a long way to the people who were watching, and Mother's hands were pressed together, while Nona pressed hers against the ilex trunk. Then, as Belinda, still looking at him, came that two feet nearer, Mr Tiffany Jones's hands shot forward, caught her in a strong grasp and in a moment she was on the fire escape with him.

Chapter 8

'No sweets for a week; bed every night at six and you are not to go out anywhere unless someone is with you. I can't trust you any more,' said Mother.

Belinda hung her head. She was very much ashamed.

'She has had a terrible fright. Must she be punished?' asked Mr Tiffany Jones.

'I'm afraid she must,' Mother said. 'Belinda has been very naughty for a long time.' And Mother doesn't know half of it, thought Belinda.

Mr Tiffany Jones was right; she had had a terrible fright.

'Perhaps this will teach you,' said Mother. 'Teach you that when you want to do things you must use a little sense.'

As long as she lived Belinda would not forget this moment when she had turned giddy on the ladder and felt herself sway. Over and over again she woke in the night and thought it was happening again, and her hands and the backs of her knees were always wet. I might have fallen and been dead, thought Belinda. One of the worst parts was that it was all of it public; everybody, everywhere she went knew how foolhardy she had been, yet it was what people did not know that tormented Belinda. Nobody knew but Nona, though Mother seemed to have guessed.

'You have told lies,' said Mother. 'Yes, even if you did not tell direct ones, you did not tell the truth and that amounts to lying. You took Little Plum, who wasn't yours; and I can guess,' said Mother, looking even sterner, 'I can guess that you have been unkind.'

Mr Tiffany Jones was beginning to guess too, yet it seemed that he still liked Belinda. 'Even after I have been such a trouble!' said Belinda. He seemed to like her – and to be a little cross with Miss Tiffany Jones. 'What I don't understand,' he said, 'What I don't understand, Belinda, is why you couldn't come and see Gem in the ordinary way.'

'Because I'm impossibly rough,' said Belinda.

'Who said so?'

'Miss Tiffany Jones.'

'Agnes? She did, did she?' said Mr Tiffany Jones.

'I try to be gentle,' Belinda explained, 'but I'm not. Nona is; she doesn't even try, because she *is* gentle. I do try but . . .' and here she was remembering knocking Gem over with her skates, and fighting, kicking and scratching on the sitting-room floor. 'Sometimes,' said Belinda in a low shamed voice, 'I'm not.'

'Well, Gem was pretty fierce,' said Mr Tiffany Jones. 'That's quite a nasty scratch you have on your cheek; and I think that I should like you to come – and so would Gem.'

But she wouldn't, thought Belinda sadly, and that was true; for all Mr Tiffany Jones's friendliness, Gem still kept her face turned away, still walked past with set lips, would not answer the most friendly smiles. Mother asked her to tea, and she would not come. Mr Tiffany Jones, they knew, had suggested they come to the House Next Door. Gem would not have them.

'You can't be surprised,' said Nona. Belinda was not surprised, and she could not forget the sight of Gem with her head down on her desk, sobbing her heart out. These things were like thorns in her mind and, 'I don't know what to do,' said Belinda. 'I would do anything if I could think of a way to make friends.'

Sometimes, when one is truly sorry and trying to make amends, a way seems to come. 'How can I tell Gem I'm sorry when she won't speak to me?' said Belinda in despair. 'How can I show her when she won't come near us? What can I do? What can I do?' asked Belinda, and then the thought came: if I were Nona, I should ask Mr Twilfit what to do.

As you know, when an idea came to Belinda, she acted on it at once, forgetting everything else. Now she forgot about not going out alone, forgot about not skating in the road near the shops and . . . I'll go at once on my roller skates and then I shall be quicker, thought Belinda. In five minutes she was standing breathless in front of Mr Twilfit at a counter piled high with books – she had left her skates outside – without waiting to say good morning, or give a word of explanation, she began: 'Mr Twilfit, you made friends with Nona when nobody else could. You understood about Miss Happiness and Miss Flower when they needed a Japanese house. You showed Nona how to make it.' The words tumbled out breathlessly. 'It was you who gave us the Japanese fairy-tale book that gave Nona the idea of Little Peach. It was you all the time, and *please* can you help me what to do about Gem and Little Plum?'

'What in thunder are you talking about?' asked Mr Twilfit.

'I'll tell you.' Belinda stood on tiptoe to lean nearer to him across the counter, and her hands happened to come down on a book that was lying there open.

'*Look* at your hands,' roared Mr Twilfit. 'Look – at – your hands!'

Belinda was too stalwart a child to be afraid of

Mr Twilfit; besides she was quite used to being scolded and she knew her hands were grubby. She remembered now that Nona always washed hers before she went to the bookshop.

'You keep your hands behind you when you come into this shop,' said Mr Twilfit, and Belinda obediently put her hands behind her. 'And talk slowly,' said Mr Twilfit, 'and don't shout.'

'Yes, Mr Twilfit,' said Belinda.

'Now you can tell me,' and Belinda began again. She began with the House Next Door, Mr Tiffany Jones and Miss Tiffany Jones, but Mr Twilfit interrupted her. 'I know the woman,' he said. 'She's a fool – wanted me to teach that poor child Latin. Go on.'

Belinda told about Gem coming and about Matson, about Gem's beautiful rooms and clothes and the pony; about how she had knocked Gem down with her roller skates, and – shamefacedly – about meeting her on the road with the class and teasing.

'Fourteen against one,' said Mr Twilfit, just as

Tom had done, and Belinda hung her head. She told about Little Plum and how she had seen her from the ilex tree; about taking over the coat and socks, the sunshade, the Japanese dinner, the quilts; reluctantly she told about the insulting messages. She grew red as she told about them, but she told. 'I think I was teasing.' She said 'I *think*' because she was not quite sure now that it was only teasing. She told about Gem's dreadful recipe and the snipped quilts and, 'H'm . . . getting fiercer,' said Mr Twilfit. When she came to the bucket of water, he said, 'Good for her,' and then Belinda's voice tailed away. She did not like to tell about the end but, 'Go on,' said Mr Twilfit. 'Let's have it all.' And in a small voice, her head bent over the counter, Belinda told.

She forgot to keep her hands behind her and one finger traced a pattern on the book she had been told not to touch, but Mr Twilfit did not interrupt her. She told about stealing Little Plum – Belinda called it stealing now – about Gem's coming and Belinda's lies – she called them lies now – of the fight and the frightening way Gem had laughed, then of how she had cried. She told of how she herself had suddenly been afraid on the ladder but of the danger she hardly said a word; it was all about Gem, and when she had finished Belinda's head was bowed low over the counter and tears were spattering down on the book. Mr Twilfit did not say a word; he only leaned forward and very gently lifted it out of the way, wiped the tears off its page with a large and yellow handkerchief, which he then passed to Belinda. 'Blow your nose,' said Mr Twilfit, and only when Belinda had blown, and wiped her eyes, did he say, 'H'm. You have got yourself into a pretty pickle, haven't you?'

The shop door opened, twanging the bell. Belinda hastily turned away to hide her face but it was only Nona. Nona had guessed that Belinda had forgotten what Mother had said about not going out alone, and had come running after her. She had seen Belinda's skates outside the bookshop and had been surprised, but now when she saw Belinda crying into Mr Twilfit's handkerchief, she guessed what had happened and quickly came to stand beside her. 'She's sorry. Terribly sorry,' Nona told Mr Twilfit.

'Yes, but I don't know how to say it,' sobbed Belinda.

Mr Twilfit cleared his throat and blew his nose on a second handkerchief that came out of his other pocket; this one had green and brown checks. The blow made a noise rather like a whale spouting, if you have ever heard such a thing. He put the handkerchief away and his eyebrows worked up and down which, as Nona could have told Belinda, meant that he was pleased, not angry. Then, 'It's always difficult to say you are sorry,' he said gently to Belinda, 'but you are lucky.'

'Lucky?' Belinda was so astonished he should say lucky that she stopped crying. 'Lucky?' she asked.

'Yes. Do you know the date?'

'The date?' This too was such a surprising remark that Nona and Belinda spoke together.

'Yes, the date.'

'It's the end of February,' said Nona and, 'Is it something to do with Leap Year?' she asked. 'But it can't be; this isn't Leap Year.'

'I'm talking about the Japanese calendar,' said Mr Twilfit. 'You say this Little Plum is a Japanese doll?'

They nodded.

'Well then, this is a quarrel about dolls, a Japanese doll,' said Mr Twilfit, 'and what better day could you have to make it up on than the Japanese Feast of Dolls?'

Belinda's head came up. Nona's face began to shine.

'Wait,' said Mr Twilfit. 'I can find you a book about it. *Japanese Festivals and Ceremonies*. It's somewhere in the office. I had meant to give it to Nona for her birthday but you had better have it now.'

Mr Twilfit rummaged in his office, then, 'Here it is,' he said and came out carrying a book that had a lantern like Gem's on the cover. He turned the leaves over until he found the right place and then began to read. 'Every year, throughout Japan,' he read, 'girls have a festival of their own. It is a Doll Festival, when big and little girls arrange ceremonial dolls in a display.'

'What are cer . . . cerry . . . dolls?' asked Belinda.

'Ceremonial dolls; grandly dressed dolls kept for special occasions. "Often they are handed down from mother to daughter for a hundred years or more,"' read Mr Twilfit from the book, '"and used only on this special day. There should be about fifteen dolls, set out on steps covered with red cloth . . ."' and he went on to read to Nona and Belinda all about the Emperor and Empress dolls, the court on the steps below them and the delicate and beautiful things that were put round them. '"Tea things, musical instruments, fans, chairs, palanquins . . . all miniature and exquisitely made of lacquer, silver or ivory, while in vases around,"' read Mr Twilfit, '"are sprays of peach blossom, the special flower of this day."'

'Blossom. That would suit Little Plum,' said Nona.

'"The Festival,"' read Mr Twilfit, '"is held on the third day of the third month." That is the third of March,' he said looking up. 'Today is the 27th of February so that is in four days' time, which would give you just time to get it all ready. I suggest,' said Mr Twilfit, 'that you keep the Festival of Dolls and that you invite Miss Gem Tiffany Jones and her Little Plum to keep it with you.'

There was a moment's amazed silence then, 'If we only could . . .' said Belinda.

'We haven't any ceremonial dolls,' said Nona.

'No emperor or empress,' said Belinda.

'We could make the steps and cover them with

red but . . . even if we could find dolls they would be terribly expensive.'

'Dolls' tables with dinners and . . . what are palanquins?' asked Belinda.

'Sedan chairs and lacquer,' Nona was saying, 'and there's no peach blossom now. Anne can make blossom with paper but would she? It's a beautiful idea,' said Nona, 'but in our house . . .'

'Your house wouldn't be suitable,' said Mr Twilfit. 'It isn't a Japanese house.'

'Then . . . ?'

'Gordon's Ghost!' said Mr Twilfit, losing patience. 'Haven't you a Japanese dolls' house?'

'Of course, but . . .' Then light broke. 'You mean . . . we should have a dolls' Doll Festival,' cried Nona and Belinda.

It was the smallest envelope Gem had ever seen; not more than an inch square, of red paper and written in writing as small as fly marks. Where the stamp might have been a white flower was painted. At the back was a gold seal, the size of a pin's head. The fly mark writing said:

'To Honourable Little Plum,
The House Next Door.'

Gem looked at it as if it might hurt her.

'Open it,' said Mr Tiffany Jones.

'It's a trick,' said Gem.

'I don't think it is,' said Mr Tiffany Jones, 'but you can't tell until you look; and it's for Little Plum, not for you,' said Mr Tiffany Jones, putting his arm round Gem. 'She can't open it herself. You must open it for her.'

Slowly Gem took the envelope up and broke the seal, which was a pity because it was so pretty; she opened the envelope flap and took out the letter, folded and about one and a half inches long. It was written in the same microscopic writing, painted with the same flower.

'"On the third day of the third month,"' read Gem in a shaking voice, '"at four o'clock in the Japanese dolls' house, Miss Happiness and Miss Flower are keeping the Doll Festival. Please, Honourable Little Plum, come and keep it with them."' Below was written 'Refreshments. Ceremonial Dress (fans should be worn). R.S.V.P.' which is what formal invitations have written on them.

'It means "Please answer",' said Mr Tiffany Jones. Below that again was written clearly: 'Please bring your most Honourable Girl.'

Gem stared at it, her eyes wide; then a flush ran up her neck to her face and glowed in her cheeks. 'Most honourable girl,' she whispered.

Chapter 9

The dolls' house had been brought down into the playroom. Nona and Belinda had cleaned it from roof to floor; clean new matting had been laid down on the floor. Nona and Melly had made new cushions and there was a third one in pale blue silk for Little Plum.

A vase of peach blossom stood in the niche. Anne had made the blossom, not of paper – that had looked too clumsy – but of peach-coloured embroidery silk in knots on the smallest of stems from a rosebush. Two other vases stood each side of red shelves, shelves like steps covered in red paper.

'What are they made of?' asked Gem, wondering.

'You will never guess,' said Belinda.

'I made them a cake,' said Nona. 'Cake cut into shapes so that I could stick the match people in.' The match dolls looked so real that from the beginning she had called them the match people.

'How could we get the dolls?' Belinda had asked Mr Twilfit at the bookshop. 'Those cere . . .' again Belinda could not manage the word, but Nona finished it for her. 'Dolls' ceremonial dolls would have to be *teeny*.'

'Perhaps I could model them,' Nona said, but had broken off. 'No, I couldn't model dolls as small as that and then there are all the clothes . . .'

'When I was a boy,' said Mr Twilfit, 'my sisters made dolls of clothes' pegs; peg dolls we used to call them.'

'Pegs would be too big,' said Belinda.

'What do your dolls use for pegs?'

'Bits of split-up matches.'

'Well then?' said Mr Twilfit and, 'Matches would do,' Nona had cried.

Mr Twilfit had been right; matches made perfect dolls'-house dolls' dolls. 'But you must be careful if you use matches,' Mother had said, 'careful not to strike them.'

'I'm not going to strike them,' said Nona. 'I need

their heads.' She had pointed the other end of each match so that, stuck in the cake, they stood upright. Then she dressed them. They looked very real. On the top step, in front of the gold paper screen, were the Emperor and Empress in robes made of gold and silver paper that stood stiffly out round them. On the Emperor's black head, for a hat, Nona had stuck a crumb of gold tinsel, while the Empress had a fuzz of gold thread. Their faces she made from the smallest blob of pinkish yellow paint. Each side of them sat a fat little dog. Nona had moulded

them from a blob of plasticine and had painted faces. 'Those dogs are called "chins",' said Belinda.

The shelf below was for the court ladies, more matches dressed in papers of ruby red, blue, purple and green. 'You know those toffees wrapped in colours – Nona used those,' Belinda explained to Gem.

On the third shelf were five musicians and here Nona had been especially clever, though Anne had had to help her. To make instruments for match people had been almost impossible, 'But Nona made them,' said Belinda proudly.

Japanese instruments are different from ours; Nona had made bamboo flutes from pine needles and fastened them to the musicians' sleeves with a drop of glue. The drum was made entirely of silver sixpences, five of them, glued one on the top of the other. 'A very expensive drum,' said Nona, 'but I'll unglue the sixpences and give them back to Mother.' The drumsticks were two pins. Mr Twilfit had shown Nona pictures of a *samisen*, which is like a banjo, and she had made two of cut-out card, painted silver with painted strings.

On one of the lowest shelves were gardeners dressed in plain red paper, tiny trees covered with more blossom, and chairs and tables cut from fine white card and painted in shining black to look like lacquer. On the tables were twisted gold paper cups and plates holding dolls'-house rice and hundreds and thousands, 'Which are the right size for dolls'-house dolls' doll's cakes,' said Belinda. They had not any sedan chairs or palanquins but they had made tiny fans and dolls'-house pots of peach blossom. It really looked like the photographs of the Doll Festival; and, 'I have never seen anything as beautiful,' said Gem.

She was a different Gem. She had come quite alone, no Matson and no shawl, though it was sleeting, and she had made Little Plum as pretty and as cared for as Miss Happiness and Miss Flower, better cared for than Little Peach. Little Plum had a new silk sash and a tiny fan, pleated with stiffened gold net. 'I pleated it myself with my doll's iron,' said Gem. She had never thought before of ironing herself.

'I think,' whispered Miss Flower to Miss Happiness, 'Miss Gem is going to be nearly as clever as our Miss Nona.'

Little Peach was allowed to come; 'Though he's a boy, he's only a baby,' Belinda had said, but they had sent Tom out.

'In Japan, boys have their own festival,' Nona had explained. 'Then they have big fish made of thin cotton or silk, lucky fish called carp. They fill with air like a balloon and the fish are hung outside the houses on tall poles. One day we'll make that festival for Little Peach,' said Nona.

There were presents for Little Plum, a new wadded scarlet jacket hanging in the shoes-off place and a pair of white socks. 'Her tanzen and her tabi,' said Nona with a shy smile. Then Belinda brought out a new sunshade, not pink with blossoms, 'We hadn't another,' said Nona. This was blue with white birds flying on it, but Gem thought it even prettier. Nona had made a second dinner tray, a black tray with red edges that held a teapot, bowls and plates, a complete dinner for Little Plum to have next day. Belinda had paid another nine pence for the tea set and Nona herself had bought a low table like the dolls'-house one, and made the cushion on which Little Plum was sitting now. Finally Nona went to the pencil-box cupboard and brought out a roll of quilts, not flowered this time but in colours of blue and white, a set of quilts and a pillow. 'A new bed for Honourable Little Plum,' said Belinda.

Melly had been asked to come and some of the girls in Belinda's class at school. Gem flinched when she first saw them but you would not have known they were the same little girls, they were serious and polite. 'We can't think what there was to laugh about now that we know Gem,' they said. Mr Twilfit came in, 'Just to look,' he said, but stayed to tea. He sat and watched them all, his eyebrows working furiously up and down. Father could not be back in time but he had given Mother 'a whole pound' said Belinda, to spend on food.

Mother had made Japanese food. It was odd

how Mother suddenly seemed to know about that. She made *sushi*, which are slices of pressed rice with all kinds of surprises in the middle – meat, shrimps, or a slice of crystallized orange, or a dab of custard with seaweed on top. 'Seaweed you can eat,' said Belinda. There were bowls of fish in sauce, bamboo shoots in syrup, rice-flower cakes in pink and white. 'Where did she buy bamboo shoots in Topmeadow?' asked Nona.

'Father must have bought them in London,' said Belinda.

'As well as the pound?' That seemed extravagant, and Father certainly could not have paid for the chopsticks Mother suddenly produced, with little tea bowls in fine china that had flowers painted on it. 'Those must have been terribly expensive. Too expensive for us,' said Nona.

'I believe,' said Belinda suddenly, 'I believe it's Mr Tiffany Jones.'

Certainly Nona had seen him talking to Mother in the road, and once, when the children were all in bed, she had been certain she had heard Mr Tiffany Jones's voice downstairs and, something is going on, thought Nona.

Just in case anyone got tired of Japanese food, there were sausages on sticks, little chocolate tarts, fruit salad, banana sandwiches and cola and lemonade to drink. 'Just in case,' said Mother.

The dolls had a feast too, in which Nona had tried to copy all the things Mother had made and filled the dolls' bowls and plates with them, and she made hot green paint-water tea to pour out of the dolls'-house teapot. Miss Happiness and Miss Flower knelt on their cushions by the tea table; Little Plum with her curved legs could only sit on hers, and Little Peach was put to crawl on the floor.

In the midst of the happiness and excitement there was a loud knock on the door and, 'Gem, will you answer it?' asked Mother.

This immediately struck Nona as odd. Belinda

was too busy handing round plates of sushi, seeing everyone had a bowl of tea, or a cola or a lemonade, to pay much attention but Nona stood still, a plate of sausage sticks in her hand; she was watching and listening. 'Gem, will you answer it?' Gem only thought Mother was making her one of the family and looked pleased and proud. She went to the door and a moment later, 'Mother!' shouted Gem in a voice as loud as Belinda's. 'Mother!'

So that's what they were planning, thought Nona, our Mother and Mr Tiffany Jones, and she, like everyone else, rushed to the door.

There was Mr Tiffany Jones, not looking sad any longer, but happy and laughing. He was pushing a wheelchair and in it, with a fur rug tucked round her knees, a deep blue coat with fur sleeves, a fur hat, sat a lady laughing. Pale green-gold hair showed under the fur of her hat, she had Gem's straight nose and grey-green eyes; her skin was pale too, but flushed now with laughing. 'May we come in?' she said, but, 'Mother!' cried Gem again and half strangled her with a big hug.

'That isn't treating her mother as a stranger,' said Anne.

Mr Tiffany Jones wheeled the chair in, and in a moment Gem's mother was surrounded by little girls. Nona, Belinda, Miss Happiness and Miss Flower were introduced: 'We made our best and ceremonial bows,' said Miss Flower, satisfied. Gem's mother was shown Little Peach, but Little Plum did not have to be introduced or shown; she was sitting on Mrs Tiffany Jones's lap.

Neither Mr nor Mrs Tiffany Jones would have known Gem; Gem with her hair flying, her cheeks pink, her eyes bright; Gem talking, snapping out remarks as fast as the other girls, Gem . . . 'Happy!' said Mr Tiffany Jones.

'I can never be grateful enough . . .' he was just beginning to say to Mother, when there was another ring at the front door – a peremptory ring – and, 'Miss Tiffany Jones has come,' said Anne in a warning voice to Mother.

A silence fell as Miss Tiffany Jones came into the room. Mr Tiffany Jones looked worried while

Gem became stiff and silent, and Belinda went and stood behind Nona. Miss Tiffany Jones's gaze went over them all, over Mr Tiffany Jones and Mrs in the wheelchair; over Mr Twilfit whom she seemed surprised to see; over Mother, Anne, the little girls, the dolls, the dolls' house and the dolls' festival, and 'Why was *I* not informed?' asked Miss Tiffany Jones.

'Informed of what, Agnes?' asked Mrs Tiffany Jones. Her voice went higher and higher. 'Gem came to this party,' said Miss Tiffany Jones, 'without my being consulted. She came without Matson or me.' But Gem had lifted her head; she was holding her mother's hand now and, 'I was asked to come with Little Plum,' she said. 'Only Little Plum.'

'Little Plum? Who is Little Plum?' asked Miss Tiffany Jones as she had asked before.

Miss Happiness and Miss Flower would dearly have loved Little Plum to sit up and tell Miss Tiffany Jones who she, Little Plum, was, but of course Little Plum had to be silent; yet Mrs Tiffany Jones seemed to understand how the dolls felt. Her finger was stroking Little Plum's topknot in a soothing way and, 'Little Plum is this little doll,' she said. 'A most important little doll who has been invited to this party with Gem – and only Gem,' said Mrs Tiffany Jones. 'We, Harold and I, came separately. It's a wonderful party and in half an hour, Agnes,' said Mrs Tiffany Jones, 'we are all coming next door for some ice cream and fruit punch. Will you be so kind as to tell Cook, Agnes? Ice cream, fruit punch in half an hour.'

Miss Tiffany Jones, Anne said afterwards, gasped like a fish, but Mrs Tiffany Jones took no notice. 'You see, you don't have to tell people when you come home,' she said. 'And I,' said Mrs Tiffany Jones, 'have come home.'

'Gem didn't smile at us because she thought we didn't smile at her. Think of that!' said Belinda. 'Gem *liked* my messages. She said they were interesting. I'm going to teach her to climb the ilex tree.'

'But not to go over the ladder, I hope,' said Anne.

'Of course not,' said Belinda scornfully.

'Gem's looking after Little Plum properly now.

Tom says he will make another Japanese dolls' house for her. I'm going to teach Gem to roller skate; she can use my skates and she says I can ride her pony. Gem says I can go next door whenever I like.'

It would have been difficult to find in all Topmeadow, or the whole of England, two happier girls than Gem and Belinda. 'We're best friends,' said Belinda.

Nona was happy too. 'All the worries and badness and teasing have melted away,' said Nona.

Miss Tiffany Jones had packed her boxes and been driven away in the Rolls-Royce. 'Forever!' said Belinda.

Though Gem's mother still could not walk and had to live in her wheelchair or on a sofa or bed, the House Next Door was changed. Mr Tiffany Jones no longer looked worried or sad and Gem was a different girl; her hair was cut so that it fell just to her shoulders and in the daytime was tied in two bunches; she wore trousers, an anorak like Nona's and Belinda's and was allowed to run in and out as she liked. Matson had left. 'I don't need someone to look after *me*,' said Gem. 'I have to look after Mother.' Miss Berryman had gone away too. Gem was going to school. 'Next term?' asked Mother.

'Next term? She's coming tomorrow,' said Belinda.

Every Friday night before dinner Father and Mr Tiffany Jones played chess, one Friday at the Fells', the next Friday at the House Next Door. Mother wheeled Mrs Tiffany Jones down to the shops; Mrs Tiffany Jones took Mother out in the Rolls-Royce. The children went to school together, spent their playtimes together, shared their friends. Gem still learned ballet, spoke French, was good at music – and had a pony; the Tiffany Joneses still had Selwyn, Cook, Eileen, a gardener and a chauffeur, while the Fells had only Mrs Bodger, but it made no difference. As for Miss Happiness, Miss Flower, Little Peach and Little Plum, they were hardly ever apart.

Each night before they went to bed they sent each other a signal. Nona would switch on the dolls' house lights; Gem would switch on her Japanese lantern. Miss Happiness and Miss Flower would come to the window and bow; Little Plum would come to hers and bow back. Belinda made Peach Boy give a little bob. 'He's too young to bow,' she said. Then she would tuck him up. Miss Happiness and Miss Flower went into their quilts, Little Plum into hers.

Then Nona and Belinda would wave their hands and put out the dolls'-house lights.

Gem would wave and put out her lantern.

'Sayonara,' was called from the Fells' house into the darkness past the ilex tree – 'Sayonara' is Japanese for goodbye. It was Miss Happiness and Miss Flower speaking, though

it sounded like Belinda and Nona.

'Sayonara,' would come back from the House Next Door. It sounded like Gem's voice, but it was Little Plum.

Have you read

With a foreword
by Jacqueline Wilson

The
DOLLS'
HOUSE

Rumer Godden